ZETA COMMANDO

REUNION WITH BIRTH MOM

BHAVNA THAKUR

INDIA • SINGAPORE • MALAYSIA

ISBN 979-8-89744-290-4

I

It was recess in the school, and Pankaj, a lively young boy, was lost in his thoughts, drifting through the haze of his subconscious mind. He couldn't stop thinking about the birthday gifts waiting for him at home and the delicacies he would indulge in later. He smiled to himself, savoring the imagined taste of cake and sweets. But the day took a terrifying turn. Gunshots shattered the school's peaceful corridors. Chaos erupted. Fear gripped his chest. His special day had become a nightmare.

His instincts, finely tuned, whispered that something was wrong. Pankaj shook his head, trying to shake off the unsettling feeling. He stood up abruptly, his heart pounding, and bobbed his head out of the door. A chill ran down his spine as he surveyed the empty corridor. Not a single soul in sight. A shiver crept up his back. His throat felt dry, his mind racing with an inexplicable sense of dread.

A chilling silence replaced the usual chatter of students. Pankaj's pulse quickened. The air felt thick, suffocating. His instincts screamed at him—run! But his feet refused to move.

Pankaj saw two tall masked figures engaged in a deadly exchange. Bullets flew in a staccato rhythm, the sound of metal colliding ringing in Pankaj's ears. His breath caught in his throat. His knees went weak. The terror that gripped him was suffocating—an iron weight pressing against his chest. He couldn't move, couldn't think. Every instinct screamed for him to run, to hide, but his body betrayed him. He stood frozen, his mind incapable of processing the horror unfolding before him.

The masked men stopped. Their heads turned toward him, slow and deliberate. A wave of pure dread washed over him as they began to approach. One of them gestured toward Pankaj with a grim smile hidden beneath the mask. It was a smile that didn't reach the eyes, a smile that promised nothing but pain.

"You're coming with us, kid," one of them said, his voice low and menacing.

Pankaj's heart skipped a beat. His legs were leaden, unwilling to cooperate, but fear—the sharp, cutting fear—forced him to take a step backward. And then another.

Before he could make a run for it, a gloved hand shot out, grabbing his arm with unyielding force. He couldn't understand how something like this was happening at his school, the place he thought was safe.

The hallways, once filled with the laughter and chatter of students, were now empty. The silence was overwhelming, suffocating. Many students and teachers were injured in the chaos, and tragically, one brave lady teacher lost her life while protecting her students.

The attackers held around 50 children hostage on the top floor of the school building, and among them was Pankaj, who was filled with fear and longing to return home. He cried out, desperate to escape, trembling as he asked the attackers: "Today is my birthday. Please let me go home. My parents and friends must be waiting for me."

One of the attackers responded coldly, "What's the phone number of your father?"

Pankaj replied, "I don't remember his phone number."

The attackers then rifled through Pankaj's school diary and found his father's number. They called home, and Pankaj's mother answered the phone.

"Happy birthday to your son," the attacker said mockingly. "We want to make his day special."

Pankaj's mother, confused and alarmed, asked, "Thank you! But I don't know who you are."

"I'm just your son's well-wisher. We'd like a birthday gift of ₹500,000 sent to his school right away," the attacker insisted.

Suddenly, Pankaj's mother went quiet, her expression crumbling in fear. Pankaj's father, noticing something was wrong, rushed over to take the phone. "Hello? Hello?" he called out, but the attacker had already hung up.

Concerned for his wife, he tried to comfort her, asking, "What's the matter?"

Despite his efforts, she remained silent, tears spilling down her cheeks. Desperate to help, he quickly dashed to the kitchen for a glass of water. He gently offered it to her, patting her back and guiding her to a chair. Gradually, Pankaj's mother regained her composure and was finally able to speak again.

"Pankaj is in a bit of a bind. It seems he may have been kidnapped. Someone called asking for a quick transfer of ₹500,000 to his school," she explained with concern.

Pankaj's father felt a wave of worry wash over him. He tried to reach out to the school office, but there was no response. Next, he contacted one of Pankaj's teachers, who sadly informed him that intruders had attacked the school premises and taken a few students hostage. In a flurry, Pankaj's parents, who were in the midst of getting ready for their son's birthday celebration, hurried to the school, leaving behind the decorations and preparations in disarray. The worried parents of other children had also arrived. The police were trying to negotiate with the attackers to safely release the hostages.

Hema, who was excited to celebrate her friend Pankaj's birthday, was spending time with her father at his supermarket. This was a common weekend routine for her – helping to organize items and manage the cash counter. Hema and Pankaj had grown close over time through their playful adventures in the park, where he lovingly referred to her as his big sister.

Later that evening, Hema eagerly asked her father if she could head over to Pankaj's house for the celebration of his birthday. Mohit, her father, paused to consider, glancing around before responding, "What time will you be home, sweetheart?"

Hema beamed, "Papa, I promise I'll be back by 6 o'clock. Can I borrow your activa scooter?"

Mohit nodded, "Of course! Just be sure to drive safely and return on time. We will go home together after your party."

"Thanks, Papa!" she replied excitedly.

Hema had a special birthday gift for Pankaj, so she hopped onto her father's scooter and headed straight to his house. Upon her arrival, she found the door locked. Curious and concerned, she started asking folks on the street for any information. When she learned about the situation at the school, her heart raced, and she dashed over there.

Once she arrived at the school, her heart sank at the sight of Pankaj's parents, their faces streaked with tears.

"Don't worry, I believe Pankaj is safe and will be home soon," Hema reassured them gently.

The situation was tense, as the intruders continued to threaten the harm of children if their demands weren't satisfied.

While discussions were ongoing, the brave police commandos were quietly preparing to take action against the attackers.

A sleek black bike screeched to a halt near the school. A figure, clad in a commando uniform, moved like a shadow, helmet obscuring the true identity. As the chaos raged, this unknown warrior scaled the building alongside elite commandos. No one noticed the silent hero slip through the smoke.

In the midst of the chaos, no one noticed this unknown hero as everyone was focused on the attackers and ensuring the children's safety. Some police officers started firing their weapons from the stairs. When the attackers noticed the police's efforts, they began firing back and locked the children in a room.

Unbeknownst to the attackers, a group of five commandos had stealthily made their way to the rooftop from the rear. The commandos on the roof quietly surveyed the situation unfolding below. As soon as the attackers were fully engaged in a confrontation with the officers on the stairs, one of the commandos hurriedly broke down the door, gently guiding the children to safety. The unknown individual wearing the commando uniform skillfully opened a window in a different room and fashioned a makeshift rescue system using a chair and some rope. They carefully assisted all the children down to a secure spot. Once the children were safe, the commandos turned their attention to the attackers.

In the fierce battle that ensued, three commandos suffered serious injuries and tragically lost their lives. During the confrontation, the unknown individual wearing the commando uniform accidentally lost her helmet. The remaining commando, Shiv Kumar, was astonished to see this remarkable fighter in action, moving with incredible bravery. He stood there, eyes wide, unable to comprehend the extraordinary scene unfolding before him.

"Hey, is that you?" Shiv Kumar exclaimed, recognizing the unknown commando. To his surprise, she was a girl he had met at a restaurant, where she had eagerly asked for his autograph, expressing her admiration for commandos. Just as the memories of their encounter filled his mind, an attacker struck him from behind, and he slowly lost consciousness.

The masked assailant lunged. She ducked, twisting effortlessly. With a sharp jab to his ribs, he staggered. In a blur of movement, she disarmed him, flipping him onto his back. His gun now in her hands, she turned, firing with precision. One by one, the attackers fell.

During the confrontation with the other attackers, the attacker chained to the window was hit by a gunshot and killed. She attempted to awaken the unconscious commando, but in vain. She left the gun with the unconscious commando, Shiv Kumar.

Her uniform was stained with blood, so she carefully changed into some clothes from the attacker's bag. Afterward, she made her way down from the back of the school building. She swiftly took off the clothes she had borrowed from the attacker's bag and washed her face and hands with fresh water from a nearby tap before heading off quietly from the scene.

The sound of gunfire had finally faded away. The injured police officers were swiftly taken to a nearby hospital, while the children, relieved and safe, had all returned home with their parents. Pankaj had made it home to celebrate his birthday, and Hema popped in to join the festivities for a little while, bringing along a thoughtful birthday gift for him.

Hema's father was patiently waiting for her to come back from the birthday celebration. When 7:00 PM rolled around and Hema hadn't returned yet, he began to feel a bit anxious. He picked up the landline phone at home and dialed, eager to hear Hema's voice when her mother answered, "Hi there! What time do you think you'll be home?"

"Hey mom, I'm just waiting for Hema. She went to a birthday party. Has she come back home?," said anxious Mohit.

"Not yet, dear. Why don't you give her a call on her mobile?" Mohit's mother asked.

"She has left her phone at the supermarket," said Mohit.

Both Mohit and his mother felt a little anxious. He wrapped up the call and tried reaching out to Pankaj's family, but no one answered. Meanwhile, the supermarket was buzzing with customers.

"Make a list of whatever you've taken from the basket and just settle the bill tomorrow. I really need to go find my daughter," Mohit said.

Just when Mohit was about to close up the supermarket, Hema walked in.

"Where have you been? I was so worried! I even called your grandmother," Mohit said.

"Dad, I'm okay! Let's chat at home," Hema replied.

With that, Mohit closed the supermarket and waved goodbye to all the customers. He and Hema then headed home, where they both enjoyed a refreshing bath before sharing a cozy dinner together.

After their meal, Mohit asked, "How was the birthday party, sweetie?"

"It wasn't that great, Dad. Some attackers held kids hostage at Pankaj's school, and he was one of them," Hema shared.

Hema recounted the whole situation at the school to her father and grandparents.

"I really wanted to join the commandos on the top floor and fight those attackers. The children were all crying, and parents were so worried. If I were a commando, I would have stood up to them and shown them they couldn't do this!" Hema expressed passionately, frustration evident on her face.

"I'm so proud of your brave spirit, but I also worry for you," Mohit said gently. "For now, let's focus on your studies. You'll have plenty of chances to help others when you're in a position to do so."

II

The police investigation into the troubling attack at Pankaj's school made a puzzling discovery: a commando uniform, stained with blood, was found on the top floor, while other clothes were scattered on the ground at the back of the building.

Remarkably, only one commando survived that harrowing incident. He is now fighting for his life in a hospital, his body riddled with wounds. The media has lovingly dubbed him the 'Zeta Commando' because a card featuring a striking Greek letter 'ζ' was found tucked in his shirt pocket.

However, the circumstances surrounding the attack remain a mystery. Eyewitnesses recall seeing shadows moving swiftly through the school corridors before gunfire erupted. Security cameras were mysteriously disabled moments before the assault. Was this a mission gone wrong, or was it an inside job?

As the lone survivor, he holds the key to the truth. But will he wake up in time to reveal it? Or will the secret die with him?

Various theories about the Zeta commando surfaced across newspapers, television debates, and online forums, fueling speculation and intrigue. The public is captivated, and law enforcement agencies are under immense pressure to decipher the mystery. Among the many theories being discussed, one has gained significant traction—both within the police force and among the general public.

According to this theory, the mysterious card bearing the distinctive Greek letter 'ζ' was not a calling card left by the commandos themselves but rather a deceptive ploy by an unknown assailant. Investigators believe that this card was deliberately placed in the pocket of the unconscious commando, possibly moments before the attacker vanished into the night. If this assumption holds true, it suggests a carefully orchestrated attempt to mislead the authorities and divert their attention away from the real culprit.

The implications of this theory are chilling. It implies that the slained commandos—highly trained and battle-hardened—were the victims of an elusive and highly skilled adversary. If an individual eliminate them, it raises unsettling questions about the nature of the assailant. Was this a meticulously planned ambush? Did the attacker possess insider knowledge of the commando's movements? Or was there a larger conspiracy at play, one that extended beyond what the police had initially assumed?

Forensic teams and intelligence agencies have been working around the clock, scouring the crime scene for overlooked clues. Every piece of evidence is being re-examined, every recorded conversation analyzed for hints of deception. The attacker's escape suggests not just skill but also careful preparation—an individual who anticipated the commando's arrival and had an exit strategy ready.

As the investigation deepens, conflicting reports have only added to the confusion. Some sources claim that there were eyewitnesses who saw a shadowy figure slipping away through the alleyways, while others suggest that the entire operation was carried out with such precision that no trace of the attacker was left behind. The authorities remain tight-lipped, refusing to disclose whether they have any suspects or leads, but their urgency is unmistakable.

The media frenzy surrounding the case has led to intense speculation, with conspiracy theories running wild. Was this an inside job? A rogue operative seeking revenge? Or is there a hidden agenda that no one has yet uncovered?

The whole investigation was painstaking. The police spent hours combing through CCTV footage from cameras positioned around the area, scrutinizing every frame for a clue. It was a slow, exhausting process, but finally, one clip stood out. The grainy footage showed a lone figure riding a custom-built motorcycle toward the school on the evening of the incident. The bike itself was distinctive—its frame modified, its exhaust custom-fitted—but the most crucial detail, the number plate, was too blurred to read.

The discovery gave investigators a lead, but not a breakthrough. Determined to uncover the truth, they broadened their search, pulling in several suspects for questioning. Among those detained were both Indian and foreign nationals, people who had been in the vicinity at the time. Some had weak alibis, others had none at all, but without solid evidence, the police struggled to build a case. Interrogations stretched into long, grueling sessions, yet the truth remained elusive.

Witness statements only deepened the mystery. Some claimed they had seen a motorbike speeding away from the school that night, while others contradicted this, insisting the roads had been eerily quiet. A shopkeeper reported seeing someone acting suspiciously near the crime scene, but when asked for a description, his recollection was frustratingly vague. The investigation was turning into a tangled web of half-truths, coincidences, and dead ends.

As the days passed, pressure mounted. The case had drawn nationwide attention, with the media demanding answers. News channels broadcast endless debates, questioning the efficiency of the police. The public was growing restless, some convinced that the authorities were covering up something bigger, others fearing that the culprit was still at large, waiting to strike again.

Faced with mounting frustration, the police turned to more aggressive methods. Desperation led them down a darker path—intensified Zeta interrogations, sleepless nights, psychological pressure. Suspects were dragged into dimly lit rooms, forced to relive the night over and over again under the watchful eyes of officers determined to extract a confession. Some broke down, admitting to things they likely hadn't done, hoping to escape the ordeal. Others remained silent, refusing to be intimidated. The line between truth and falsehood blurred as exhaustion set in.

Yet, despite their relentless efforts, the case refused to yield its secrets. The figure in the CCTV footage remained a shadow—unknown, untraceable. The motorcycle, which should have been a crucial clue, led to nothing. And the real perpetrators, whoever they were, seemed to have planned their moves meticulously, leaving behind no clear trail.

With every passing day, the frustration within the police force grew, but so did the unease among the public. Whispers of police brutality and false accusations began circulating, threatening to shift the focus away from the crime itself. Was justice truly being served, or had the investigation become a desperate chase for a scapegoat?

III

An insightful private detective, Dipankar Agarwal suggested a different angle, proposing that the culprit might even be a girl, especially since a lady's handkerchief with stitching HV was discovered on the top floor. He believed that this potential escapee was overlooked in the police investigations.

His suspicion deepened when he spotted Hema Verma in the school attack footage. He had known Hema and her family for years, yet something about her presence in those clips unsettled him. Then came the handkerchief—embroidered with the initials HV. It was a small detail, but to him, it was damning. Could she really be the elusive assailant? The thought sent a chill down his spine. If his instincts were right, then the truth was far more shocking than he had ever imagined.

Dipankar's unease grew as he shared his suspicion with his wife, showing her the school attack video. The missing commando fought with remarkable agility and precision, moving with a skill that seemed oddly familiar. His mind flashed back to an incident at a cafe, where Hema had effortlessly handled a group of unruly boys. The way she moved, the sharpness of her reflexes—it was too much of a coincidence. Could it really be her?

"Hema is a bright and cheerful girl," Dipankar said thoughtfully. Everyone in her community adores her. Raised by her devoted father, Mohit Verma, she has always been a mix of mischief and discipline. Mohit often reminds her, "Nothing is perfect in this world, and striving for perfection isn't necessary." She lives by that wisdom, embracing life as it comes.

Dipankar visited Hema's home to find out more. He discovered that Hema's world was full of warmth, not just from her father but from her beloved pets—Pitu the parrot, Titu the dog, Micu the cat, and Sqilu, the playful squirrel. These pets brought an additional sense of warmth and playfulness to her home, and often Pitu would tease her grandparents, calling them funny names. It was a lively, loving atmosphere.

Dipankar further discovered that while Hema adored her pets, her true passion lay elsewhere. Sports—especially taekwondo had always been her first love. She was sharp, competitive, and effortlessly graceful.

Recently, she had finished her senior secondary school with outstanding achievements. Her fascination with the police and defense jobs had always been present. She had also spent her school years training as an NCC cadet, gaining valuable skills that would shape her future. Her father and grandparents supported her wholeheartedly, encouraging her to chase her dreams, whatever they might be.

Mohit told Dipankar about Hema's recent visit to her school and the unexpected cafe incident that followed.

On a special day, Hema returned to her school to collect her senior secondary marksheet. Nostalgia washed over her as she ran into old classmates, and together, they decided to catch up over coffee at a nearby cafe. Laughter filled the air as they reminisced, sharing dreams and aspirations over snacks. The warmth of the moment, however, was soon interrupted.

A group of boys from a nearby school entered the cafe, their initial remarks seemingly harmless—casual teasing tossed their way. But the comments soon escalated into taunts, growing bolder with each passing minute. The girls tried to ignore them, hoping they would lose interest, but things took a turn when one of the boys began throwing paper balls at their table.

Frustration simmered. Hema's friends were ready to leave, but she, always the composed one, chose to confront the situation.

"Is there a problem?" one of the boys in her group asked, his patience wearing thin.

"Yes, there is," a boy from the other group smirked. "Do you have a solution?"

Then, one of them pointed at Hema. "Tell that girl to be my girlfriend," he said, his voice dripping with arrogance.

Hema raised an amused eyebrow. "Me?" she asked, her lips curling into a half-smile. "And why exactly should I?"

Her friends tensed. The boys in their group stood up, but a quick glance around confirmed the grim reality—they were outnumbered. Fear crept in as the situation grew more unsettling.

"Let's call the police," one of Hema's friends suggested.

Hema, however, remained unfazed. "No need," she said calmly. "Let me handle this."

"Are you going to stand up for them?" one of the troublemakers mocked.

"We're not looking for trouble," Hema replied, her voice steady. "Just leave us alone."

One of the boys stepped in front of her, blocking her way. "Where do you think you're going, sweetheart?" he sneered.

Hema sighed, shifting the bag on her shoulder. "Step aside," she said, her tone firm.

The boy laughed. "Make me."

In the blink of an eye, Hema seized his collar, twisted her body, and slammed him onto the cafe floor. The room gasped in collective shock. The other boys barely had time to react before she turned her attention to them. A swift kick sent another stumbling into a table. Every move was precise, controlled—a testament to years of taekwondo training.

The cafe, once alive with chatter, fell into stunned silence as the boys crumpled one by one.

The commotion attracted the cafe owner's attention, and he quickly called the police. Officers arrived to find the dazed boys sprawled across the floor. Witnesses recounted the scene, still in disbelief. The boys were taken into custody, their parents notified.

Through it all, Hema remained composed, her calmness contrasting sharply with the chaos around her. She had resolved the situation in a way no one had expected.

That day, those in the cafe saw a side of Hema they never knew existed. The quiet girl who adored her pets had just single-handedly taken down a gang of bullies. And with that, the mystery of who she truly was began to unravel.

Dipankar shared his suspicion with Mohit. "It might just be a coincidence, but the elusive assailant in the school siege fought with such precision, such skill, that it reminded me of Hema."

IV

Hema had always felt a special connection to the Greek letter 'ζ', as she wore a locket shaped like it around her neck. While she didn't know much about this cherished locket, she recognized it as part of her identity.

Her father, Mohit Verma, used to bring her exciting fictional books featuring superheroes and introducing her to action-packed TV shows and movies, like those with commandos, avengers, and heroes such as James Bond, Harry Potter, Superman, and Spiderman etc. Among her childhood favorites were the animated series Zeta Project and Zeta Squad. Hema often pretended to be the main character of the Zeta Project Infiltration Unit Zeta, a humanoid robot who went on brave adventures.

When Hema learned through the news channels about a real-life Zeta commando, who was the only survivor of that recent attack on the school, she excitedly asked her father if they could meet him. After a bit of effort, they tracked down the commando's address, hopeful to meet Hema's hero. Unfortunately, they were told he was in a coma and unable to receive visitors.

Feeling a bit disheartened, they returned home, but Hema held onto hope, wishing and praying for her hero's quick recovery. She repeatedly checked in with her father about how the unconsious commando was feeling for many days. Each time, he would reassure her that he would be alright soon, and then they could visit him together. From what Mohit had learned about similar situations, he felt deep down that Shiv Kumar might struggle to return to his usual self again. But he kept this worry to himself for Hema's sake.

When Hema finally lost hope for his recovery, she ceased asking her father about his health and focused her energy on preparing for her upcoming NDA exams and SSB interview.

As the government prepared to honor brave individuals during the Republic Day celebrations, one of the awards was for the unconscious hero, Shiv Kumar, who had captured the attention of both media and police as the 'Zeta Commando'. Hema and Mohit attended the Republic Day festivities, hoping to see the Zeta commando, but when his wife received the award, Hema felt a wave of sadness wash over her.

After months of battling various health challenges, the unconscious commando began to show signs of improvement. Though he was still unable to speak, he found a way to communicate by writing notes with his injured right hand. His handwriting was a bit shaky, making it hard to read. Only family and a few close colleagues had the privilege of visiting him during this time, while the media still waited for their chance. His family helped him understand that he had received a bravery award from the President of India for his courageous actions during the school attack.

One of his colleagues shared that he had gained fame as the 'Zeta commando' because of a special card with a Greek letter 'ζ' that had been found in his pocket. Instead of feeling proud, he found himself feeling puzzled. Lost in his thoughts, he remembered a charming girl he'd met in a restaurant who had asked for his autograph on a card featuring that same Greek letter 'ζ'. He felt a spark of excitement and tried to express that a girl had been the true hero, saving the school children and him during the school incident.

However, he quickly realized that speaking was still out of reach. He attempted to communicate through his notes that he is not elusive Zeta commando; rather, it was a young girl who deserved the recognition.

His colleagues gently inquired, "What exactly happened that night?"

Through his notes, Shiv Kumar opened up about an unexpected truth: It was a remarkable girl, who bravely rose to the occasion and saved the children that night. With her superhero-like courage, she took down all the attackers and even came to his aid. Unfortunately, he was struck from behind by one of the assailants and lost consciousness, leaving him unaware of the remarkable events that unfolded afterward.

This new revelation from Shiv Kumar about the real Zeta Commando made its way into the media, sparking a renewed effort among private detectives, reporters, and police to locate the brave missing person from the school incident.

The mystery deepened as Shiv Kumar's disclosure indicated that the person they were searching for was a girl who had displayed extraordinary heroism by saving the children and standing against their attackers. It brought forth several intriguing questions that needed addressing:

1) Is the missing individual a daring rescuer or someone involved with the attackers?

2) If she was indeed one of the attackers, what could have motivated her to save the children?

3) Why would someone who heroically saved lives choose to remain hidden?

The private detective, Dipankar Agarwal, who had suspected that the escaped individual could potentially be a girl, gained public recognition following the news that emerged from Shiv Kumar's notes. To bring this mysterious figure to light, the police collaborated with a talented sketch artist to create a depiction of the girl based on Shiv Kumar's description. Despite their efforts, police and detective agencies were still on a quest to uncover the true identity of the incredible Zeta commando who resembled that sketch.

V

The following year, in February, Mohit and his family were thrilled to set off on a trip to Goa. He reserved two cozy rooms at a lovely hotel for their stay by the beach. Hema could hardly contain her excitement as it was her very first train journey. Once they boarded the train in the evening at their local station, they settled into their comfy seats.

Once they arrived at the Goa station, they hopped into a taxi that whisked them away to their hotel. In the afternoon, they made their way to the Arjuna Beach.

Hema and Mohit took to the waves, enjoying exhilarating jet ski rides and breathtaking parasailing, which left Hema mesmerized by the thrill.

The next day, the vibrant Goa carnival filled the city center with energy and excitement. People were dressed in all sorts of playful costumes, and Hema proudly wore her lion-faced head cap, adding to the fun.

As the carnival flowed with colorful floats and cheerful music, people lined the streets, soaking in the festivities. Hema's heart swelled with joy as she took in the beautiful display of Goan culture.

Suddenly, someone in a wolf-faced head cap bumped into Hema from behind, causing her to stumble and letting her phone slip from her pocket. In a flash, a boy grabbed her phone and dashed away.

"Hey! Thief! Someone stop him!" Hema cried out, sprinting after the thief.

In a twist of fate, a girl in the crowd, wearing a lion-faced costume just like Hema's, bravely intercepted the thief. She confronted him with a swift slap, retrieving Hema's phone, and demanded to return everything he had stolen during the carnival.

As Hema approached, eager for her phone back, the girl stared at her, awestruck. It felt like looking into a mirror; Hema's face was a reflection of her own.

"Thank you so much!" Hema exclaimed, reaching out her hand for a friendly shake with the girl.

The girl shook Hema's hand gently but seemed momentarily lost for words, just gazing at Hema with wide eyes hidden beneath the mask.

Hema felt a bit taken aback by the girl's silence.

"Hey! Is everything alright?" Hema inquired softly.

After a moment of surprise, the girl finally spoke, "Oh my goodness! How can this be?" She paused, curiosity evident in her voice. "What's your name?"

"I'm Hema Verma," Hema introduced herself with a warm smile.

"I'm Aamiya George," the girl replied, her voice brightening.

"No need for thanks! We all have a part to play in helping our community. Bad things shouldn't go unchecked," Aamiya added with determination.

"Are you a police commando? Can I see your face?" Hema asked playfully.

"Oh dear, I completely forgot about this silly mask!" Aamiya chuckled as she unzipped her disguise.

When Aamiya revealed her face, Hema's eyes widened in amazement, leaving her momentarily speechless. Her breath hitched as she stared at the girl in front of her. Same face. Same eyes. Same everything.

Aamiya tilted her head. "Are you...?"

"I don't know," Hema whispered. Her hands were shaking.

Aamiya's eyes flickered with something... hope? Fear? She swallowed.

Hema couldn't shake off the feeling that Aamiya could be her long-lost sister who was somewhere with her mother.

"Do you live with your mother?" Hema gently asked.

"Sadly, I don't have a mother. I live in an orphanage," Aamiya replied, her voice tinged with sadness.

The carnival music blared in the background, but in that moment, it was just the two of them.

"I should be on my way now. My parents will start to worry," Hema said with a hint of urgency.

"Okay, take care of yourself," Aamiya said warmly.

"You too!" Hema replied, blowing a playful kiss before heading off.

Once they returned to their hotel in the evening, Hema excitedly recounted the interesting encounter to her family, sharing her surprise at meeting a girl who looked so much like her, aside from her hairstyle.

"She could be my sister!" Hema exclaimed with excitement.

"Where exactly did you meet her?" Hema's grandma inquired, her interest piqued.

"I spotted her at the carnival. We both were just as shocked to see each other," Hema explained animatedly.

"Sometimes, people can look like famous actors or sports stars, but that doesn't necessarily mean they share a family connection," Mohit offered with a reassuring smile.

"You know, I've often heard our elders say there are seven people in the world who look just like each other," Mohit's father remarked thoughtfully.

"I felt such a special connection when I shook hands with her," Hema expressed, her eyes shining with excitement.

"Don't worry! If you bump into her again, take her home address. We can visit her parents to uncover the truth," Mohit suggested encouragingly.

The next day, Mohit's family set off to explore more of the beautiful sights in Goa. While they were at one of the tourist attractions, Mohit and his parents stepped into the washroom, leaving Hema outside, where she suddenly spotted Aamiya.

"Hi there! You from beautiful Goa?" Hema inquired Aamiya, her smile radiating warmth. "I'd love to hear about your parents."

"Actually, I'm here with my friends. Sadly, my parents passed away in a car accident, so I'm living at an orphanage," Aamiya replied quietly.

"I'm really sorry to hear that," Hema said sincerely.

"Your name sounds European. Are you Christian?" Hema asked curiously.

"Yes, I am Christian, but I'm not from Europe," Aamiya clarified gently.

"That's wonderful! I'm from Kurukshetra in Haryana," Hema responded, her face lighting up.

"Which state are you from?" Hema inquired with genuine interest.

"I hail from Punjab, which is right next to your state of Haryana," Aamiya shared.

"I need to head out now; my friends are probably waiting for me at the city center," Aamiya said, looking a bit hurried.

"When you're back home in Punjab, please do drop by our place in Kurukshetra. I would love to see you!" Hema called out as Aamiya began to leave.

"Absolutely, I'd love to visit you!" Aamiya replied cheerfully before disappearing to meet her friends.

As Mohit and his parents emerged from the washroom, Hema excitedly shared, "She just stepped out to meet her friends at the city center!"

"Who just left?" Mohit asked, sounding curious.

"Aamiya, the girl who looks so much like me!" Hema exclaimed, beaming with joy.

"She's from Punjab. I invited her to visit us in Kurukshetra. She's been through a lot, losing her parents in a car accident and growing up in an orphanage," Hema explained warmly.

After an unforgettable time in Goa, Mohit and his family happily boarded the train, reminiscing about their adventures on the way home.

VI

After a year of diligent preparation, Hema successfully cleared the NDA examination and was selected for the SSB interview. Her father, Mohit, had made arrangements for their travel by booking air tickets for both of them. However, on the day of their scheduled flight, he encountered pressing work commitments that could not be postponed.

Initially, Mohit considered the possibility of rescheduling his assignments and even suggested that Hema cancel her travel plans. Despite this, Hema was eager to attend the SSB interview and endeavored to persuade her father and grandparents of her ability to take the journey independently.

"There are several other candidates from our city participating in the SSB interview," Hema stated.

Hema also expressed her commitment: "I have dedicated the past year to preparing for this NDA examination and SSB interview. Please allow me to face this opportunity."

After a moment of reflection, Mohit recalled various instances where Hema had competently managed responsibilities on her own, including cooking, participating in sports tournaments, and excelling in her studies.

Ultimately, he agreed, stating, "Alright, I will take you to the airport."

Hema responded with gratitude, saying, "Thank you, Pa. I appreciate your support," and embraced her father in a warm hug.

Mohit, accompanied by his parents, went to the airport to drop off Hema for her flight. As they bid farewell during the check-in process, Mohit embraced Hema warmly and kissed her on the forehead, marking the first time he would be apart from her since he discovered her as a newborn baby near a bridge. It was a poignant moment for him, and he expressed his emotions, saying with teary eyes, "All the best, my Tiger."

Hema responded, "Thank you, Pa. Please take care of yourself and ensure you eat properly every day. I will check your weight when I return home."

After checking in, she entered the airport, while Mohit and his parents patiently waited outside until her airplane took off. This marked Hema's first experience at an airport, which filled her with excitement.

Once on the plane, Hema contacted her grandmother on phone. "Grandma, it is so beautiful," she exclaimed.

Her grandmother playfully responded, "Really! Is it the airport or the airplane?" before wishing her well with her SSB interview.

A bit fatigued from a lack of sleep over the past few days, Hema soon fell asleep after the plane's takeoff. However, during the flight, two individuals dressed in black began to behave aggressively toward a middle-aged couple. When the flight crew intervened, the assailants became increasingly violent and revealed they were carrying dangerous items. One hijacker managed to enter the cockpit, declaring the airplane had been hijacked, while another held the elderly man from the couple and threatened his safety.

Hema awoke to a tense atmosphere filled with fear.

"What happened? Is there a problem with the airplane?" she inquired of the surrounding passengers.

Before anyone could respond, one hijacker approached her aggressively, threatening her with a sharp object.

In response to the chaos, a male member of the elderly couple shouted, "Hey! Leave the girl," and threw a small pillow at the hijacker in an effort to protect her.

The hijacker retaliated by slapping the elderly man, but Hema, drawing on her karate skills, bravely intervened. She quickly overpowered the hijacker, throwing him on the floor and restraining him with the assistance of other passengers. Together, they secured him to an unoccupied seat and used tape from her bag to silence him.

When another hijacker emerged from the cockpit, he called out to his accomplice, who was tied to a seat. In a fit of anger, he demanded to know who had restrained him and attempted to free him. Hema, seated nearby, intervened by grabbing the hijacker by his hair and striking him. A struggle ensued between Hema and the hijacker, prompting several young passengers to step in, successfully subduing him and securing him to a seat as well.

The scene left everyone on the flight in disbelief. They erupted in applause for Hema, celebrating her courage.

"You are a true hero! We are so proud of you," remarked a senior flight attendant.

"What is your name?" inquired an elderly couple.

"Zeta Commando," she replied playfully. "Commando! How wonderful. Your parents must be so proud," the elderly gentleman remarked.

"Where are you traveling alone?" asked the elderly woman.

Hema smiled and responded, "I am traveling to attend an SSB interview."

Upon learning that the flight was redirected due to the hijacker threat, Hema urgently requested, "Please take the airplane to the scheduled destination of Bhopal airport. I have my SSB interview and cannot afford to be delayed. Please, I implore you."

A senior flight crew member informed the pilot that the hijackers had been subdued by passengers and tied to their seats. The crew member urged the pilot to proceed to the original destination due to Hema's important engagement. The pilot consented and announced that the plane would return to Bhopal airport, albeit with a delay of approximately thirty minutes, much to the passengers' relief.

Police were stationed at the airport in anticipation of the situation. Upon the aircraft's arrival, they boarded and arrested both hijackers. In the meantime, Hema discreetly exited the terminal and took a taxi to her pre-arranged hotel. Once all passengers had disembarked, many began to search for Hema, unaware that she had already departed.

"They were misbehaving and had threatened the passengers aboard the plane. A group of young individuals gained control and secured them," explained the elderly couple to the authorities. "Please ensure they are apprehended; they are dangerous."

After the police had escorted the hijackers away, someone approached the elderly couple and asked, "Why did you not inform the officers about the brave young woman? She deserves commendation and recognition for her exceptional handling of the situation."

"Indeed, she is a courageous individual," affirmed the elderly gentleman. "However, she was en route to her SSB interview. We feared informing the police would cause her to miss it."

Hema had requested both the flight crew and the elderly couple to refrain from disclosing her identity to the authorities, as it could jeopardize her chances of attending her SSB interview.

The male member of the elderly couple expressed, "We hope she receives her recognition from God. We desire for her to become a true commando."

This prompted a curious inquiry from him: "Was she not a commando?"

This individual was a private detective who gleaned from media reports that Shiv Kumar had indicated in his written notes that Zeta commando is indeed a girl.

Reflecting on the possibility, he speculated that this young woman could be the one he sought. Frustrated by what he perceived as a missed opportunity to gather more intelligence about Zeta commando, he began to kick the ground in agitation.

He then inquired of the elderly couple and other passengers, "Does anyone know about the girl who confronted the hijackers?" However, everyone declined to provide any information regarding her whereabouts, acknowledging only a recognition of her face. Each co-passenger expressed admiration for Hema's courage and extended their best wishes for her future endeavors.

VII

Hema navigated her SSB interview with confidence, successfully passing each stage. However, despite her strong performance, she was not shortlisted in the final selection. Though momentarily disheartened, she chose to view the experience as a valuable learning opportunity.

Upon returning home, a wave of disappointment washed over her, but she quickly redirected her focus toward preparing for the NDA examination. Her father and grandparents reassured her that setbacks are merely stepping stones to success and advised her to give her best effort, leaving the outcome to fate.

One afternoon, as Hema played chess with her grandfather, her grandmother busied herself in the kitchen preparing snacks. Meanwhile, Mohit had stepped out to visit the supermarket. As she contemplated her next move, curiosity sparked within her.

"Grandpa, how did you and Grandma meet? Was it an arranged marriage?" she inquired, her eyes twinkling with interest.

Her grandparents exchanged a knowing smile before her grandmother spoke. "We both came from humble, middle-class backgrounds. Though we attended the same college, our real bond developed during our B.Ed. studies at an education college. However, our journey was not easy—our families initially disapproved of our relationship. For a while, we lost contact, though we silently kept track of each other's lives."

Her grandfather picked up the story. "Fate had its own plans for us. Years later, we unexpectedly reunited during a teaching job interview. Overcome with emotion, we talked for hours, finally admitting our true feelings. We decided to approach our families again, this time with the security of employment on our side. Thankfully, we both secured the jobs, and with that, our parents granted their blessings for our marriage."

Hema listened intently, fascinated by their journey. "That's incredible! You both must have been so relieved."

Her grandmother nodded. "Starting our life together was a beautiful phase. We settled into our new home and even had a pet cat. A few years later, Mohit was born. He was an earnest, well-behaved child who loved playing with the cat. Bright and diligent, he eventually cleared the entrance exam for a prestigious engineering institute and pursued a B.Tech in mechanical engineering. We worried about how he'd adjust to living away from home, so I took a three-month leave to help him settle into hostel life."

"I remember that," her grandfather added. "Once he grew comfortable, formed friendships, and adapted to his studies, your grandmother returned home. We remained in close contact with him and soon found ourselves engaging in motivational speaking at educational events to keep ourselves occupied."

Hema beamed with admiration. "That's amazing! I'm so proud of both of you."

Her grandfather sighed, his tone turning somber. "We had hoped Mohit would take up a job after his B.Tech, and he did secure a position through campus placements. However, he soon became dissatisfied with the corporate culture and resigned within a few months. With our financial support, he pursued his dream of starting his own business—manufacturing electrical appliances like fans, coolers, and air conditioners. The venture showed promise at first, but he struggled with cost management and ultimately faced bankruptcy."

Hema's expression grew concerned. "That must have been devastating for him."

Her grandmother nodded. "It was. But we reassured him that failure is often a stepping stone to success. We encouraged him to remain positive and consider alternative career paths. Look at Thomas Edison—he failed nearly a thousand times before successfully inventing the light bulb. Every setback is an opportunity to learn."

Her grandfather added, "We urged him to focus on personal development rather than just financial gain. If you build your skills, success will follow naturally."

Hema absorbed their words thoughtfully. "And then he decided to prepare for civil services, right?"

Her grandmother's eyes softened. "Yes, but despite his hard work, he couldn't clear the exam. His repeated failures took a toll on him, and he sank into depression. He withdrew from his friends and became isolated. Whenever he met relatives or acquaintances, they would ask about his job and marriage, which only deepened his distress."

Hema hesitated before asking the question that had been lingering in her mind for years. "Grandma, may I ask you something?"

"Of course, my dear. You can ask me anything," her grandmother replied gently.

"What happened to my mother? Has she…passed away? Or did she leave us for some reason? Papa never talks about her."

Her grandmother's face momentarily clouded with hesitation. After a brief pause, she spoke carefully. "You were born during one of the most difficult periods of Mohit's life. Your arrival brought him light during his darkest days."

Hema was startled by her grandmother's words. Before she could ask further, the front door creaked open, and Mohit stepped inside, bringing the conversation to an abrupt halt.

"Is there anything to eat? I'm starving," Mohit asked his mother.

She smiled, quickly placing a plate of popcorn and snacks on the table. "I prepared these for you."

Mohit and Hema sat together, enjoying the popcorn in comfortable silence. After a few bites, he turned to her. "How was your day? How's your exam preparation going?"

Hema brightened. "Everything is going well! Today was my rest day, though. I played chess with Grandpa—we had two draws, but I lost the third game. I'm determined to win next time."

Mohit chuckled. "That's the spirit. Keep challenging yourself."

Later that evening, they took a leisurely stroll in the park. As they walked, Mohit shared valuable insights on interview preparation. "Confidence is key, Hema. Maintain eye contact with your interviewer—it conveys self-assurance and respect."

Hema listened intently, absorbing her father's advice. Despite the uncertainties ahead, she felt motivated, ready to tackle whatever challenges life had in store for her.

As they walked home, Hema felt a newfound sense of determination—not just for her NDA preparation, but for uncovering the missing pieces of her past.

VIII

The details surrounding the Zeta commando remained enigmatic for a considerable period until the police team investigating the school attack noticed a photograph featuring a young girl who bore a striking resemblance to the sketch of the so-called Zeta commando.

A photographer, who happened to be a close friend of one of the police officers involved in the investigation, hosted a birthday celebration for these officers one evening. Following the festivities, one of the police officers requested the photographer to share his latest images on his laptop. The collection included captivating photographs of nature, animals, and wildlife.

During their viewing, they noticed a young girl in one of the photographs, who closely resembled the sketch. She was with a dog and a cat in a park. The police officers endeavored to identify the park and carefully reviewed the photographs multiple times. They unanimously agreed that the park was likely situated within the city, and they became convinced that the girl was indeed the same individual as in the sketch. They expressed their gratitude to the photographer for his assistance.

The following day, the police initiated searches in various parks across the city.

One day, Hema was walking her dog in the park when she noticed a police van parked near the entrence of the park. Two officers stepped out, scanning the area. She didn't think much of it – until their eyes locked onto her.

The officers walked toward her.

"Excuse me, miss," one of them said, his voice calm but firm. "What's your name?"

"Hema Verma," she replied, gripping her dog's leash a little tighter.

The officer exchanged glances with his partner, "Do you mind answering a few questions at the police station?"

Hema's stomach twisted. "Is... something wrong?"

"We believe you might be connected to an ongoing investigation," the second office said, his tone neutral, unreadable. "We'd like to ask you a few things."

Hema forced a nervous chuckle. "I—I don't understand. What investigation?"

The first officer pulled out a folded piece of paper. He held it up, and Hema's breath caught in her throat. It was a sketch of her face... or at least, someone who looked exactly like her.

Her heartbeat pounded in her ears.

"Do you recognise this person?"

Hema swallowed hard. The sketch was eerily same, but there was one difference... the girl in the drawing had short, boyish hair.

"I... no, that's not me," she said quickly.

The officer studied her carefully. "You're sure? This girl was present during a high profile school attack last year. She fought like a trained commando—took out attackers and disappeared before we could identify her.

Hema felt her chest tighten. She knew what police officers were talking about. She had been there that night. But admitting that would be dangerous.

"I—I don't know anything about that," she said, trying to keep her voice steady.

The second officer glanced at her neck as if searching for something. "Do you have any scars or injuries? Something from about a year ago?"

Hema's mind flashed back to the school attack—to the sharp, burning pain she had felt that night.

The officer sighed. "Alright. But we still need to speak to your parents. Can you take us to your home?"

Hema's hands felt clammy. She had no choice. "Okay... let me call my father first."

As she walked toward her house, her mind raced. What if they found out she was there that evening?

Hema invited the police officers to enter her home; however, they declined, stating they would remain in their vehicle.

Concerned, Hema contacted her father, asking him to come home immediately. Mohit, feeling anxious, promptly closed his supermarket.

Upon his arrival, he noticed a police van stationed outside his residence, which heightened his worry. Hema also came outside to join him.

"Good afternoon, Inspector. May I inquire about the situation?" Mohit asked one of the officers.

"Please don't be worried. We've been searching for a person for the past year, and we believe we've found her today. That individual is your daughter," the officer responded.

In a state of concern, Mohit turned to Hema and asked, "Have you been involved in something unlawful?"

"Papa, I am completely unaware of anything," Hema replied.

"I am struggling to understand. Could you clarify the situation?" Mohit asked the police team.

"Do you recognize this girl?" one officer inquired, presenting a sketch.

After examining the sketch closely, Mohit fell deep into thought. Finally, he responded, "She resembles my daughter, but I don't recall her ever having such a hairstyle."

Hema's mind flashed back to her encounter with Aamiya in Goa. She had such boyish hair.

"Please try to recall if you ever had this particular hairstyle," the police team encouraged Hema.

"I have never had this kind of boyish haircut," Hema insisted.

One of the police officers informed Mohit that this sketch is of the elusive hero, the real Zeta Commando. Mohit grew suspicious due to Hema's presence that evening, as she had previously informed him that she was there. He was also reminded of past memories, recalling that Hema had always been fascinated by the Greek letter 'ζ' since her childhood and was an avid fan of the TV series, Zeta Squad and Zeta Project.

Additionally, he recalled Hema's words from that evening after returning from her birthday party, where she expressed that if she had been a commando, she would have taken on the attackers and taught them a lesson.

Mohit suspected that she might have worn a boy's haircut wig during such a confrontation. Mohit looked at Hema in disbelief, to which Hema responded with a disapproving shake of her head.

"Can we meet the commando who survived the attack?" Mohit inquired of the police team.

"Yes, that would be advisable," a policeman replied.

The police team escorted Hema and Mohit to Shiv Kumar in the hospital. The hospital room was quiet except for rhythmic beeping of machines. Shiv Kumar, still weak but alert, sat upright in his bed. His sharp eyes followed the police officers as they entered with a young girl.

Hema saluted him instantly. Respectfully. As if she had admired him for years.

Shiv Kumar's heart skipped a beat. Something about her felt familiar.

The officers placed a sketch on the table beside him. "Is this the girl who saved you?"

He glanced at the sketch. The short hair. The fierce eyes. The unmistakable presence of a warrior. His fingers trembled as he reached for it.

"It's her, isn't it?" one officer pressed.

Shiv Kumar looked at Hema again. Her hair were different— longer. Her neck was clean, no scar. But her face...

"No. It wasn't her."

His breath hitched. His mind spun back to that night— gunfire, chaos, a shadow moving with lighting speed, a girl fighting like a trained commando.

His eyes locked onto Hema's, searching. Looking for an answer.

"It's not her," he whispered hoarsely.

The officers exchanged confused glances. They returned with Mohit and Hema to investigate further for any mysterious elements within their residence. Upon searching Mohit's house, they found no suspicious items, only an extensive collection of books.

The police team told Mohit that they have to come to the police station whenever they were called for any questioning. "We are so sorry for any inconvenience."

This police team told this whole incident to their senior police officer. After a long discussion, the officer decided to conduct a DNA test and match it with the DNA of the sample taken from the abandoned commando uniform found in that attack.

Hema was called to the police station and her sample was taken for a DNA test. After a few days, the DNA test report came.

Hema was called again to the police station for interrogation.

A police officer studied the DNA report, then looked up at Hema.

"It is match." he said.

Silence filled the interrogation room. Hema blinked, her mind racing. How could this be?

Mohit sat beside her, his fingers clenched into a fist. "That's not possible," he said firmly.

The officer leaned forward, "Then explain this..." He pulled out the blood-strained commando uniform found at the crime scene. "This belonged to missing Zeta. And now we have the proof that Zeta is sitting right in front of us."

The police team again contacted Shiv Kumar.

"Hema's DNA matched the blood found on the commando uniform," an officer added. "It has to be her."

Shiv shook his head. "No... something is wrong."

Her DNA matched. But she didn't have the scar on neck. The missing Zeta commando must have an injury scar on her neck.

His gaze darkened with understanding, "She is not the one who saved me, Her twin sister is."

Hema's breath caught. Her twin? The Zeta Commando?

Memories of Aamiya flashed through her mind—her identical face, her fierce presence, the strange feeling of familiarity when they met.

It all made sense.

"Do you have twin, Hema?" one officer asked cautiously.

Hema swallowed. "Did she?"

She turned to her father, who had been silent this whole time. "Papa..."

Mohit looked away, pain flashing in his eyes.

The police contacted a group of doctors at a hospital. They presented the sketch, photos of Hema, and DNA test results to the doctors. Based on the DNA tests and images, it seemed that both belonged to the same individual.

However, the police then informed the doctors that the sole witness from the incident indicated there must be a noticeable injury scar near the neck of the girl in the sketch. Although they had located a girl who resembled the sketch, she bore no neck injury.

The police team asked, "Is it possible for two individuals to share the same face and DNA?"

"Yes, it could happen in the case of identical twins," one of the doctors replied.

The police summoned Mohit and Hema to the hospital. A group of doctors examined Hema and confirmed there was no injury scar around her neck.

A police officer inquired of Mohit, "Do you have twin daughters?"

Hema began to suspect that her mother might have taken her twin sister away to live elsewhere.

Mohit instructed Hema to wait outside and then informed the police that he was not married and Hema was his adopted daughter. He was unaware whether Hema had a twin sister or not. He shared that he had adopted her from a hospital, providing the address where Hema was treated after he discovered her near a bridge.

The police team visited that hospital in the city but were unable to verify the birth of any identical twin girls approximately 20 years ago. Ultimately, the police showed the sketch to the hospital staff.

A nurse commented, "This girl came to the hospital about a year ago. She had injuries and a large cut near her neck. We treated her for that wound, but she vanished the next day without notifying anyone."

The police are now convinced that Hema has an identical twin sister.

"If you ever learn anything about her twin sister, please inform us right away," one policeman told Mohit.

They permitted Hema and Mohit to return home. Hema became eager to learn about her mother, as only she could reveal the truth about her twin sister.

Hema found herself deep in thought about Aamiya, whom she had met in Goa. She had a suspicion that Aamiya might be her twin sister.

IX

One day, Mohit and Hema were at home together. Mohit's parents had attended a motivational event for school students that day. Mohit chose not to open his supermarket on that day. He was explaining some physics concepts related to stress and strain to Hema.

"Pa, what does depression mean? How can we tell if someone is experiencing depression attacks?" Hema inquired of Mohit.

"Only God knows the precise answers to these queries. It occurs when it needs to happen. Sometimes it is difficult to prevent. You may find yourself a victim of depression attacks without realizing it," Mohit replied.

"What situations can lead to depression attacks?" Hema continued.

"It has happened to me as well. Based on my experience, I would say that when things don't unfold as we hope or when we refrain from discussing our problems with friends and family, we are more likely to encounter depression attacks," Mohit explained.

"Pa, could you share how it happened to you?" Hema asked.

"It's quite an extensive tale. You might find it dull," Mohit said.

"Pa, please, I genuinely want to know. Grandma also mentioned that I was born during that time you faced depression. I am eager to learn what happened to my mother during that period," Hema insisted.

Upon hearing that his mother had shared something with Hema about her birth, Mohit felt perplexed and uncertain about his response. He had always told Hema the truth and encouraged her to do the same. After a long pause, Mohit decided to disclose the truth behind his depression and her birth.

Due to some setbacks in his life, he was feeling quite down. His parents were worried for his health. They took him to a psychiatrist.

One day, he was looking for someone to talk. His parents were not at home. He decided to go to the market and wandered around there. Suddenly, he heard someone shout, 'Hey Mohit!' He looked around in surprise and saw Tanya, one of his classmates from college, waving at him.

Mohit felt a wave of happiness at having someone to talk to. He and Tanya approached each other, shook hands, and exchanged greetings.

"How are you, Mohit? Is everything allright?" inquired Tanya.

"Yes, everything is OK," Mohit said. "How about you?"

"I am doing well, too," Tanya replied. "What a surprise to see you after all these years!"

They went to a Starbucks cafe. They bought coffee and nibbles before settling up at a corner table.

"What's bothering you?" Tanya questioned.

"I'm not pleased with myself. I don't understand why," replied Mohit.

"Look at me. I'm not employed either. I had a job but left because it didn't suit me. Life throws unexpected things our way. But everything happens according to His plan (pointing her finger upwards). So, try to stay cheerful." explained Tanya.

"I truly appreciate your advice and encouragement," Mohit replied.

"God has blessed us with this beautiful life. It's our duty to keep it joyful," Tanya remarked.

"By the way, if you don't mind me asking, where's Sumit? Do you still keep in touch with him?" Mohit asked Tanya.

Summit was one of their classmates in the college.

Tanya became slightly emotional and remained silent for a moment. After some time,

"He has moved to America for his master's program. Initially, after he went to America, we stayed in touch for a couple of months. Now, we haven't spoken in a while. I noticed on social media that he has made some friends there. He seems to be happy now," Tanya responded.

After their encounter, Mohit and Tanya began talking more frequently over the phone. Mohit felt like he was developing a special connection with her.

Although Mohit and Tanya didn't see each other for several days, they stayed in touch through phone calls. Feeling quite happy, Mohit began to prepare for the civil services exams again, as it was what his parents wished for him. His parents were quite pleased with how Mohit was doing.

He took the preliminary examination but didn't make it to the main examination, which made him quite upset. He tried to reach out to Tanya, but she had stopped communicating with him. She had blocked his number, and he felt completely dejected.

He attempted to discover the reason for her silence and visited her house, but her parents told him she had gone to America. He was filled with anger and disappointment, shunning conversation with anyone.

His parents became anxious and concerned about his well-being. One morning, when his parents left for urgent errands,

"Mohit, I have prepared food for you. It's in the kitchen. After you bathe, please eat and take it easy today. We'll return in the afternoon," said Mohit's mother.

After his parents left, he awoke feeling so troubled that he considered ending his life. He looked around the house for something that could help him, but when he found nothing, he went to the nearby train station with intentions of jumping in front of an oncoming train. However, he was turned away because he didn't have a ticket for the station.

He felt rage and headed directly to a bridge over a nearby river. It was cloudy morning, and the light near the bridge was dim. There was no one present. He considered it the ideal spot to jump into the river and end his existence.

As he was about to leap, he heard a loud cry of a newborn baby. He paused and scanned the area. He couldn't see anything. Attempting to jump again, he heard the same cry once more. He also noted the barking and commotion of dogs. Suddenly, all his anger vanished. He hurried towards the bushes to discover what was happening. He spotted some dogs fighting. Grabbing a stick and some stones to scare them off, he approached.

When all the dogs fled, he noticed a small, shiny basket adorned with decorations. He was astonished to find a tiny baby inside. He opened the basket, and the baby appeared to be struggling to breathe. Taking the baby in his arms, he concealed the infant under his clothing and dashed toward the road. He hailed a taxi and arrived at a hospital. He went directly to the emergency room. A nurse took the baby from him and began administering oxygen. Once the baby started to cry, she summoned a doctor. The doctor arrived, examined the baby, and instructed the nurse to take the baby for immediate treatment.

After some time, a nurse stepped out and said, "You arrived just in time; otherwise, you could have lost your baby. You need to pay ₹50,000 for your baby's treatment."

Mohit began to cry and found himself unable to speak for a moment. "Can I see the baby?" he inquired.

"Of course. You can go inside to see her," replied the nurse.

Mohit entered the room to see the baby and gently placed his hand on her forehead, saying, "I will care for you. You are my little tiger."

"Thank you very much, sister," Mohit expressed his gratitude to the nurse while folding his hands.

"What happened? Where is her mother?" the nurse questioned.

Mohit wept again and struggled to find words for a while.

"Alright! The baby needs to be breastfed," the nurse said.

After a long pause, Mohit replied, "Is there any alternative to feed her? Her mother is no longer with us."

"Oh! I am very sorry," the nurse responded. "Please deposit ₹50,000 at the reception and bring these items."

The nurse handed Mohit a lengthy list of items. He returned home and arrived there in the evening. He found his parents upset and crying.

"We tried calling you, but we realized that you had left your phone in your bedroom. What is wrong with you?" his distressed mother said.

"Have you eaten? Where were you all day? Your phone is on the table in your room. We have no idea what is happening with you," his emotional father added.

Mohit broke down in tears. After a while, he said, "I will explain everything, mom. Please give me ₹50,000. I need it urgently."

"My son, that's not a problem. You can take as much as needed. But let's discuss the issue you're facing. Are you in serious trouble?" his mother inquired.

"No trouble, mom. I have to go to the hospital right away. I'll return home in the morning," Mohit insisted.

His parents were taken aback by his words. They were perplexed and worried, fearing he might be in significant trouble.

"You say there's no trouble, yet you're insisting on going to the hospital. There must be an issue. Just tell us. Maybe we can help you find a better solution," his anxious father said.

"Pa! I want to share everything, but it will take time to explain the entire situation. Right now, I need to get to the hospital. She urgently needs me," Mohit replied.

This situation became a mystery for his parents. They considered the possibility that it might involve his girlfriend, who was hospitalized.

"Is your girlfriend sick and in the hospital?" his worried mother asked.

"Yes, mom, please give me ₹50,000 and let me go now," Mohit pleaded.

She urged Mohit to eat something before heading to the hospital.

He headed back to the hospital, picked up the items from the list provided by the nurse.

After confirming that everything was alright with the baby, Mohit returned home next morning. His parents asked Mohit about her health.

He said, "She's perfectly fine. She's such a delightful girl."

Hearing this, his parents felt joy, thinking he might have started dating. They were eager to learn more from Mohit. "What does she look like? Who is she?"

Mohit hesitated for a moment, taking a deep breath before speaking.

"I'm not sure how you will take this, and I don't even know how to handle it myself. I have a baby girl," Mohit stated.

"A baby girl? Are you referring to a girlfriend or something similar?" asked Mohit's father.

"Dad, she's a tiny newborn baby," Mohit explained.

"What are you talking about?" his father replied, confused.

"Is this baby from your girlfriend or what? We can't understand you," his mother said.

"This baby was in big trouble. I found her by chance. She's not from any girlfriend or anyone else. This baby saved your son, mom," Mohit revealed.

Overwhelmed with emotion, he began to cry as he continued,

"It's hard for me to explain, but the truth is that I was so upset and depressed that I thought about ending my life by jumping in front of a train or off a bridge into a river," said Mohit.

Upon hearing this, his mother slapped him in anger.

"Did you not think of us for even a moment?" she shouted, tears streaming down her face.

Mohit also started to cry uncontrollably.

"I'm really sorry for what happened. I was overwhelmed by many things not going my way. But now, I feel completely okay," Mohit reassured them.

"How old is the baby?" his mother asked.

"I'm not sure, but she's probably just one or two days old," Mohit answered.

"Have you lost your mind? Are you serious that a two-day-old baby saved you?" his father asked in frustration.

Mohit explained the entire incident in detail. Now, his parents felt convinced and at ease.

"She is like a goddess to us. She has given Mohit a new lease on life. We will call her Hema (Hey Ma)," his mother declared.

His parents informed a doctor about what had happened and their desire to adopt the baby. This doctor, a family friend and a doctor at a government hospital, advised them to follow the official procedure for the adoption. After the baby recovered and all the necessary legal steps were completed, they brought her home.

X

Mohit's life now revolved around caring for his baby. This has restored joy in his life. His parents were happy to see him actively involved in her care.

"Believe in yourself, son. You're a skilled engineering graduate, and I have no doubt you'll make the right choices. You can achieve wonderful things in life, and I'll always be here to support you," his father said with a warm smile.

Mohit embraced his father tightly and replied, "Thanks, Dad! I have a dream of opening a supermarket."

To start with, Mohit opened a grocery shop in the city center. With dedication and hard work, he transformed his grocery shop into a bustling supermarket within two short years. This newfound success allowed him more time to care for his beloved Hema. Occasionally, she would join him at the supermarket, and he felt a surge of joy watching her play.

Mohit lovingly called Hema by playful nicknames like "Tiger," "Commando," and "Joker." By the time she turned three, she was already attending a lively sports academy where she enjoyed trying out various sports.

Hema started going to a school and quickly made a wonderful group of friends. After a few years, she curiously asked Mohit one day, "Some of my friends have mamma who comes to school for parent-teacher meetings."

Mohit gently explained that all children have mamma.

He found himself at a loss for words when it came to answering her questions about her mother. He shared his thoughts with his mother.

She responded, "We knew this day would eventually come."

Mohit's parents gently encouraged Mohit to consider getting married so that Hema could also have a mother figure in her life.

His parents began a heartfelt search for a girl who would warmly embrace Hema as her own daughter. It was quite a challenge for them to explain Hema's situation to others. For a year and a half, they faced difficulties in finding the perfect match for Mohit that they truly wished for.

One sunny day, Tanya came to the park and sat down on a bench. While playing joyfully in the park with other children, Hema noticed a young girl sitting alone on a bench, looking quite downcast.

"What's got you feeling so sad? Did you lose something special?" Hema asked with genuine concern.

Tanya turned to Hema, pulled her into a hug, and after a moment, replied, "Thank you, sweet girl. You're absolutely adorable."

With a big radiant smile, Hema cupped Tanya's cheeks and said, "You're adorable too! You don't look as beautiful when you're sad." My papa always tells me, "Be happy and spread happiness. If you see someone feeling down, do your best to lift them up."

Tanya instantly felt a special connection, as if Hema had been her friend for ages.

She felt a wave of emotions wash over her and tears began to flow. She felt such a deep bond with Hema that her thoughts drifted to her daughter, whom she had lost shortly after her birth.

Tanya loved visiting Hema often and cherished their conversations in the park.

One sunny afternoon, while they were chatting, Tanya asked, "What about your papa and mamma?"

Hema replied, "My papa runs a supermarket, but I haven't met my mom. My grandma says she had gone to meet God on another planet."

Feeling overwhelmed, Tanya wrapped Hema in a tight hug, unable to find the words. Tanya felt a wave of emotions and tears welled in her eyes, which she tried to conceal.

One day, Hema's grandparents strolled into the park as Hema and Tanya were deep in conversation. Hema happily introduced Tanya to her grandparents, and they all quickly felt at ease with one another.

Hema's grandparents became fond of Tanya within a few weeks and imagined her as a wonderful daughter-in-law, though they were a bit shy about saying it.

Hema couldn't stop raving about her wonderful friend, urging her dad to meet her. Her enthusiasm genuinely made him eager to see her friend.

One sunny Sunday, as fate would have it, Mohit met Tanya at the park.

"Hey Tanya, what a delightful surprise!" exclaimed Mohit.

"Hi! It's so great to see you after a long time," replied Tanya with a warm smile.

"So, when did you come back from America?" Mohit asked, genuinely curious.

"What do you mean? I never went to America! I've been right here in India the whole time," Tanya replied, looking a bit puzzled.

"Really? You didn't go to America!" Mohit said, slightly surprised.

"Nope, not even once! I've been here, but things got really complicated for me. I stopped being in touch because I found out I was pregnant with Sumit's baby. You remember Sumit, right? We were together before he headed off to the USA. Deciding whether to keep the baby or not was incredibly tough since I still held onto hope that Sumit would return," Tanya shared with a deep sigh.

"Wow, I had no clue! I even tried to visit you after you stopped talking to me, but your parents said you were away in America," said Mohit.

"Oh no, that wasn't true. My parents were really worried because of my pregnancy. They were likely more concerned about their reputation than my situation. They pressured me to consider aborting the baby, and it put a lot of strain on me. They even distanced themselves from their relatives during that time. Honestly, this whole experience was quite overwhelming until the baby finally arrived," Tanya explained, her voice tinged with emotion.

After sharing some joyful moments together, they decided to head home. Mohit and Tanya started chatting more often on the phone, and their meet-ups became a regular joy in their lives.

Mohit's parents were delighted to learn that he and Tanya were keeping in touch.

Mohit's mother had hopes that Mohit would consider proposing to Tanya one day. She believed Tanya would be a wonderful partner for him and also a caring mother for Hema.

One sunny day, as Mohit and Tanya chatted in the park, Tanya curiously asked, "If it's alright to ask, what's the story with Hema's mom?"

Mohit was caught off guard and hesitated to respond.

Tanya gently continued, "It's perfectly fine if you'd rather not say. Hema mentioned her mom had gone to God, so I just wanted to know."

After a moment, Mohit said, "To be honest, we're not really sure who her mother is. I like to think I got Hema from God."

Tanya asked, "Did you adopt her from an orphanage or something?"

Mohit maintained his belief that he received her from God. Tanya found his response puzzling, but she didn't want to press on; she respected his silence.

"I was hurt by my ex-boyfriend, which led to me having a baby girl. Sadly, she didn't make it, as my family and doctors informed me. Sometimes, I feel like my parents might have kept some truths from me about my daughter. Still, it was thanks to my parents that I managed to overcome the darkness of depression and anxiety," said Tanya.

Tanya lives with her parents and works as a computer teacher at a school, even though she held a B.Tech in computer science. She had the potential to land a lucrative job at a top company, but she grappled with depression and anxiety due to her past struggles.

Nevertheless, she found joy in teaching her students about computers and coding, and most of them truly enjoyed her classes.

One sunny day at the park, Hema's grandma spotted Tanya after quite some time, and they immediately greeted each other with warm hugs. They both exchanged heartfelt wishes about their health and chatted about their daily lives. Grandma, with a gentle smile, asked Tanya, "Do you like Mohit? You know, he's such a shy guy who often struggles to share his emotions."

Tanya, her eyes sparkling, replied, "Oh yes, I've had a soft spot for him since our college days. He's such a sincere and wonderful person."

Grandma, her excitement bubbling, suggested, "What if we talk to your parents about the idea of you marrying Mohit?"

For a brief moment, Tanya was taken aback, speechless by the unexpected notion.

With a gentle tone, she responded, "I didn't mean to imply that I liked him in that way. I'm a bit surprised to hear this. We share a lovely friendship. I once had a boyfriend who didn't treat me right, and that relationship led to me having a child. Mohit knows about everything that happened with me."

Grandma, her heart aching with concern, exclaimed, "Oh my goodness! I'm truly sorry to hear that. I had no idea."

Feeling a wave of disappointment wash over her, Grandma lost herself in her thoughts for a moment. Then, with kindness in her voice, she reassured Tanya, "You know, regardless of this situation, we all truly cherish you, and so does Hema. I thought you would be perfect for Mohit, and you'd take such lovely care of Hema. We've met several girls over the years, but none compared to you in warmth and compassion towards Hema. I hope you don't hold this against me. I'm just worried for both Mohit and Hema."

Tanya gently replied, "Please don't apologize. I care deeply for both him and Hema, and I would love to be a part of their lives. But I'm afraid that Mohit might not want to marry me after knowing about my past."

Grandma, with an encouraging smile, responded, "I've seen how much he clearly cares for you. Don't worry – I'll have a chat with him."

One afternoon, Mohit called Tanya on her phone.

"Mohit here! I've got something important to share with you. Could we meet up today, or if you're free, swing by my supermarket?"

Tanya felt a bit puzzled, suspecting that Mohit's mother had mentioned something to him. She wondered if this meeting was about marriage and what she would say if he proposed.

After several gentle nudges, Tanya agreed to meet him at the park. In the evening, Mohit arrived at the park with Hema, who joyfully played with her friends.

"For the past few days, Hema has been calling mamma in her dreams. My mom thinks you know who Hema is calling her mamma. I'm more than willing to bring her home if she can take care of my little tiger," Mohit said.

Tanya responded thoughtfully, "I'm not sure how I can assist you with this. I don't know who she might be."

Mohit sighed a bit, "I was so hopeful that you'd help me with this, but now I'm confused about why my mom thought you could assist in bringing her home. I'm really sorry for taking up your time."

Tanya smiled warmly, "Don't worry about it, Mohit. You're still just as I remembered you from our college days. I think your mom might have meant something else. She did ask me about our marriage a short while ago."

Mohit's eyes widened, "Oh my goodness! What are your thoughts on that?"

Tanya replied with a bright smile, "I wouldn't mind at all if you feel the same way."

Mohit's parents then met with Tanya's family. They were pleased with the prospect of Mohit and Tanya getting married. Both families began to plan a charming wedding celebration. However, one day, Tanya's father came to visit Mohit's dad to chat about the wedding arrangements. When he encountered Hema, an unexpected twist occurred, he was taken aback to learn that Hema is actually Tanya's daughter!

Spotting the beautifully crafted locket adorning Hema's neck completely threw him off balance, and he felt a wave of anxiety wash over him. He became entangled in thoughts, fearing that Tanya might discover the truth about her daughter and harbor negative feelings towards him.

Overwhelmed, he hurriedly left Mohit's house without saying a word. Everyone at Mohit's place was puzzled, searching for him. Mohit decided to reach out to Tanya to see how her father was doing. Tanya informed Mohit that her dad was home but seemed withdrawn.

"Did anything happen?" she inquired.

He rejected the idea of marriage for Tanya and Mohit. Everyone was caught off guard by his sudden decision. He claimed he consulted an astrologer who warned him that Tanya is Manglik, suggesting their union could bring misfortune, potentially harming one of them.

When Mohit's parents learned about Tanya's Manglik status, they too grew uninterested in the idea of their marriage. Still, Mohit couldn't shake the recurring dreams where Hema lovingly called out for her mom. He resolved to talk to Tanya's dad.

The following day, he visited Tanya's home, but neither Tanya nor her mother were present; her father was alone. Mohit earnestly sought out Tanya's father, pleading for support in their marriage.

"I'm truly excited about the possibility of marrying Tanya, even though she's considered Manglik. I've made this decision for my daughter; it's important for her to have a loving partner who can care for Hema as if she were her own daughter. Hema shares a strong bond with Tanya and knows her very well, which is a comforting thought for me," said Mohit.

"My greatest worry is that my daughter might come to resent me one day. I can't bear the thought of losing her; she means the world to me. She is my only child, and my love for her is immeasurable," Tanya's father stated.

"I'm not sure I follow you. How could she possibly hate you after marrying me? Losing her doesn't make sense to me – she's a wonderful girl, kind, respectful, and caring towards everyone," explained Mohit.

"You might feel differently about Tanya once you learn more about her past. She has had a baby with her boyfriend, and I fear how that will impact everything," Tanya's father explained.

"Tanya has already shared her past with me, and it hasn't changed my feelings for her. I truly admire her and wish to spend my life with her," Mohit stated.

"I made a terrible mistake with her daughter, Hema," Tanya's father confessed, his face clouded with regret.

Mohit's breath caught. "What? Hema is Tanya's daughter?" His mind reeled, as if ground beneath him had shifted.

Tanya's father lowered his gaze. "I was misguided and foolish... blinded by own fears. I abandoned her near a bridge shortly after she was born, believing I had no other choice. But when I saw the locket she wore—the one crafted by a goldsmith—I knew the truth. My heart sank."

In his effort to ensure the baby would be cared for, Tanya's father prepared a beautiful basket and adorned it with lovely gold jewelry, hoping someone would see it and take her home. He even added a uniquely designed locket to help him recognize her if fate ever brought them together again. How comforting it would be to know she was safe.

He intended to leave the basket at the temple gate, but when the moment arrived, his heart couldn't take it. Instead, he placed the basket with the precious baby near a bridge under the cover of night.

The following evening, he returned, worried yet hopeful to see if someone had taken her home. To his shock, he discovered the empty basket and the gold jewelry strewn about, but the baby was nowhere to be found. For a brief moment, he feared the worst, thinking that perhaps wild animals had harmed her. He searched around, but there was no sign of her anywhere.

Now, after discovering that the baby was doing well, he felt an immense sense of relief and happiness wash over him. Still, a wave of fear and concern swept through him at the thought of losing his only child, Tanya. He couldn't help but feel that Tanya would despise him when she learned what he had done to her little one.

Emotions overwhelmed him, and he felt on the verge of tears. Mohit, seeing this, chose not to press the matter any further. He headed home, returning to his daily routine, though a hint of disappointment lingered in his heart.

Upon learning about her being Maglik, Tanya also decided not to push for her marriage with Mohit. Gradually, life began to settle back into its usual rhythm following this unsettling incident. They all found their way back to their everyday lives, and regular communication became less frequent.

Hema immersed herself in her schoolwork, making plenty of friends along the way. At home, she was happily occupied with her assignments and enjoying time with her pets.

In the evenings, she excitedly joined a sports academy where she explored various sports. Mohit encouraged Hema to take up taekwondo and learn valuable self-defense skills. She participated in both school-level and national-level sports events, and there were even times when parents of her male classmates playfully complained about Hema beating their kids.

XI

After listening to her father's heartfelt story about her birth and life journey, Hema felt a swell of pride for Mohit. She wrapped her arms around him and said, "I love you so much, Pa. You're my hero."

"You are my everything, my darling. You've shown me how to embrace a beautiful life. You're my little tiger," Mohit replied. "I can't wait to see you as a real-life commando."

Mohit had a strong belief that Hema would always put her heart into everything she pursued. During her second attempt at the NDA and SSB interview, she was thrilled to be selected for the Army Wing of NDA. While happy, Mohit also felt a flicker of anxiety, realizing that Hema would be away for a few years studying and training.

Hema noticed the tension etched on her father's face, and deep down, she worried that he might struggle with depression again once she began her training and eventually started her career in the defence services.

"Pa, how about we take a stroll in the park?" Hema suggested.

After a moment of silence, Mohit asked, "What did you say, Hema?"

She gently repeated, "Come on, Pa, let's go to the park for a walk."

As they walked through the park,

"Pa, you don't seem happy," Hema asked as they went through the park.

"Who says I am not? I'm perfectly happy," Mohit said. He tried to put up a strong face, but his sadness was obvious.

"Pa, you might say otherwise, but your face tells a different story," said Hema.

"I just need to learn how to cope without my beloved tiger by my side," Emotional Mohit said.

"Oh, Pa, no one can truly separate us except for God. I'm fulfilling your dreams, and I will become a real-life commando," Hema stated.

"I can hardly express how proud I feel, but as any father would be, I'm worried too," Mohit exclaimed.

"Pa, I have to go over to see Tanya and her parents," she remarked.

"Why do you feel the need to go there?" Mohit inquired.

"Oh, Pa, don't worry about it. Please let me go," Hema pleaded.

A wave of nostalgia rushed over her as she remembered portions of her childhood, albeit she didn't fully recall Tanya. When Hema arrived at Tanya's home, she was surprised to see the old couple she had encountered in an airplane-hijack incident.

"Hello! Is this where Tanya lives?" Hema asked.

Grandma turned and, surprised, recognized Hema right away.

"What a wonderful surprise! How did you find us?"

"Hello, Grandma & Grandpa! It's wonderful to see you!" Hema said. "How have you been?"

"We're doing fine, thank you. And how about you?" Grandpa stated.

"I'm fantastic, too! It's wonderful to see you both after so long," Hema added.

"So, how was your SSB interview?" Grandma enquired.

"I felt great about my SSB interview, but I didn't make the final merit list. This year, I gave it another go, and guess what? I was selected! Soon, I'll be leaving to begin my training," Hema said. After a while,

"Why are you looking for Tanya?" Grandma inquired.

"I have something vital to discuss with Tanya and her parents," Hema stated.

Grandma inquired, "Do you recognise her parents?" with a big smile on her face.

Hema seemed confused and eventually asked, "Are you Tanya's parents?".

"Yes, sweetheart. We are her parents," Gradma said.

"Oh my God! It appears that fate continues bringing us together, which must mean something fantastic. I found out from my father that I am your grandchild," said Hema.

"Oh, who is your father? And where is he now? I believe there is a mix-up here," Grandpa replied.

"My father is Mohit Verma, the man your daughter was supposed to marry. But you were worried about how she'd react if she found out the truth about me, so you declined," Hema explained.

Grandpa hurriedly seeks the locket around Hema's neck. He is taken away by what he sees and sinks back into his chair.

"I share responsibility for what you've gone through. A nurse once told me about your grandfather's plan to leave you at a temple or with a childless couple, and I regret not stopping him," said Grandma.

The grandparents hugged Hema warmly, feeling an unbreakable kinship.

Just then, Tanya returned home and overheard their heartfelt conversation through the window. Overwhelmed with emotion, she absorbed the truth about Hema and rushed inside, embracing her warmly.

Hema, too, was overcome with emotion, tears streaming down her cheeks. They hugged for a long time in silence before Hema finally spoke.

"Did you know I am your daughter?"

"How could I have known?" Tanya replied, her voice thick with emotion. "But knowing it now is the most precious moment of my life, my Tiger."

Tanya smiled through her tears. "How are you, my sweet Teddy Bear? I always believed, deep in my heart, that one day you would find me. I just never expected it to take so long."

Tanya's father sat in stunned silence. Disbelief washed over him as he buried his face in his hands, tears glistening in his eyes.

"Tanya, she's the brave girl who saved us during that hijacked airplane incident," Grandma interjected proudly. "She fought like a commando. She even cracked the NDA exam. In just a few days, she'll be starting her training."

Tanya turned to her father, disappointment evident in her voice. "Pa, I am extremely disappointed. Why did you do this to us?"

"If you don't mind, I'll get straight to the point. I came here to ask if you are ready to marry my father," Hema said to her Mom.

Tanya was taken aback by Hema's words. She fell into deep thought before finally responding.

"I don't know what to say right now," she admitted. "But I was ready to marry your father years ago… and I am still ready now, my Teddy Bear." A soft smile crossed her lips. "But it would be lovely if you could speak to my parents first."

Tanya's parents happily supported her decision to marry Mohit. Tanya, her parents, and Hema decided to pay Mohit a visit at his home. When they arrived, Mohit and his family were pleasantly surprised to see all of them together. After exchanging warm greetings, they settled comfortably on the sofas in the living area. Mohit went into the kitchen to whip up some tea and grab a few snacks, while Tanya followed him to lend a hand.

"What is going on? Did Hema convince you all to come here? You know, my tiger has successfully qualified for NDA and will begin training in just a few days," Mohit said.

"Yes, I am aware that she is beginning her adventure with her studies and training at the defence Academy. I couldn't be more proud of her, but let's be honest: she's our tiger. You knew the entire story of Hema, but you kept it from me," Tanya said. "I feel betrayed by all of you, including my own parents, for keeping her away from me for so long."

"I only knew about Hema from your father. This was the reason he refused your marriage to me. Your father didn't want to tell you the truth about Hema because he was scared you would resent him for it," said Mohit.

"Why don't you head back out? I'll take care of things in your kitchen," remarked Tanya.

"Thank you so much," Mohit said, pulling Tanya into a warm embrace.

Meanwhile, Tanya's parents took the opportunity to speak with Mohit's parents about the situation and expressed their support for the marriage. It was a delightful moment for everyone involved.

When Mohit exited the kitchen, he was greeted by the cheerful expressions of both his and Tanya's parents. Realizing everyone was on the same page, he respectfully touched the feet of Tanya's parents and said, "I can't thank you enough."

"We truly apologize for everthing, and we're so grateful to you for looking after Hema," Tanya's father replied, his heart filled with gratitude. "You've helped lift a heavy burden off my conscience, and I deeply regret any pain this may have caused. I'm truly sorry for everything."

A few days later, Mohit and Tanya celebrated their beautiful wedding filled with joy and laughter. Hema was absolutely delighted with how everything turned out, feeling liberated from any worries about her father, excited to embark on her NDA training journey.

Not long after, everyone gathered at the railway station to send Hema off. It was bittersweet, filled with both smiles and a touch of sadness.

XII

Hema was excited to start her NDA training, which promised to be quite challenging. Nevertheless, she couldn't be happier – this was the disciplined life she had always dreamed of. In the defence academy, she enjoyed playing badminton with her batchmates and made sure to call home regularly whenever she found a moment.

After a wonderful semester of training, Hema was overjoyed to spend a month with her family back home. It felt so special to be reunited with her parents after such a long time apart. Everyone in their community beamed with pride at Hema's accomplishments. To celebrate, Hema and her family enjoyed some delightful hikes together, soaking in the beauty around them.

One sunny day during her vacation, a troubling event occurred: two young girls from Hema's village suddenly went missing. A report was filed at a nearby police station, but despite the police's efforts, they couldn't locate the girls.

Hema later discovered that a senior police official may have been involved in their disappearance or was aware of their whereabouts. She paid him a visit at his home, determined to learn more about the missing girls.

"Do you know two girls have gone missing in our town?" Hema questioned the police officer.

"Who are you? How do I know about it? Go out of here immediately," He replied aggressively.

Hema remained calm and solid, smiling warmly. Just as it appeared he was about to strike out, she firmly grasped his collar and gently instructed him to keep his cool, warning that if he didn't, things would get serious.

The police officer refrained from attacking Hema because he believed she was too strong to manage. After a while, she sat on the couch and asked the officer about his daughter. He became worried and immediately tried to contact his wife.

His wife had gone to her mother's house with their daughter. Nobody answered the phone. He called again, but no one answered.

"If anything happens to my daughter, I will kill you," the police officer said fiercely to Hema.

"The parents of those girls cherish their daughters in the same way that you adore your daughter," Hema explained.

The police officer calmed down and provided information on the missing girls.

"A local politician's son intended to marry one of the girls, but she denied his proposal. He attempted to frighten and persuade the girl. He also asked her friend (the second missing girl), to help persuade her to marry him. He had kept the girls in a secluded spot on his personal farm," the police officer explained.

"I'm capable of confronting this politician's son and bringing the girls home," Hema stated. "But I wouldn't do it since we have police to deal with such situations."

Hema softly reminded the police officer of his pledge when he joined the police force. The police officer was motivated by Hema and resolved to free those girls from the politician's son's captivity.

When the police officer arrived at the farm, he found the girls tied up. He asked that the girls be released because the consequences would be far worse. The politician's son hit the officer and chastised him with various insults.

He hesitated to respond. Meanwhile, Aamiya showed up. The officer mistaken Aamiya for Hema. He drew his gun and shot one of the politician's associates in the leg.

"I'll handle it; you set the girls free and take them home," Aamiya said to the officer.

One of the politician's companions lunged toward Aamiya. He hardly had time to blink before Aamiya grabbed his collar, twisted her body, and shoved him to the ground. The other buddy ran forward, but she was faster. One well-placed kick drove him staggering back and falling into a table.

She treated each of the companions in the same manner, surprising both the police officer and the politician's son..

The police officer took the girls home. Parents were pleased when they finally saw their daughters. The parents of those girls showed their appreciation with folded hands. "Thank you very much."

The officer was taken aback to see Hema and said, "Do you have a twin sister?"

"How did you know it?" asked surprised Hema.

"She fought like a commando with the politician's associates and helped set the girls free," the officer said. "For a moment, I thought that it was you."

"She is Zeta Commando," Hema said.

"Is she still there? I want to meet her. Please proceed to that location," said Hema.

They went there, but Aamiya was not present.

After one month of vacation, all NDA cadets returned to the academy. Hema got busy with her training and studies. At home, Mohit and Tanya learned that they were expecting their first child. However, they decided not to tell Hema because she would become sidetracked from her studies and training.

One day Grandma informed Hema that she will have a sibling by the time she return home the next time. Hema became really excited after hearing that. She was overjoyed for her father because he had begun a new life, something she had always desired for him.

The next day, Hema called her parents, anticipating them to give her good news regarding her sibling. They didn't tell her anything, but instead kept asking about her studies and training.

Mohit didn't grasp what Hema meant when she mentioned hiding something.

"Hey my tiger, do you think I can do it with you?" Mohit asked Hema.

Hema grew skeptical that her grandma had informed her about the sibling based on her suspicions, and there could still be no news about her sibling

"Pa, in my dream yesterday, I saw that I had a sibling," Hema stated.

"Okay, my dear commando. I'm so sorry. This is true. We didn't want to tell you since it would distract you from your studies," Mohit said.

"All good, Pa. Grandma informed me yesterday. I was simply joking about my dream," Hema said. "Take care of mom, Pa."

"How is mom? Can I talk to mom now?," Hema asked.

"Yes, certainly," Mohit said.

Hema spoke with her mother for about 10-15 minutes, expressing her happiness. Tanya grew distraught and advised Hema to take care of her while she concentrated on her training.

"You are our commando. You have to do your best. We are incredibly proud of you," Tanya stated.

After finishing three semesters, Hema took a month off and went home. Her sibling had already been born by then. It was a boy. She enjoyed playing with him. One month passed rather quickly.

Hema successfully completed her NDA training and received best cadet award.

Her parents attended her convocation ceremony. They were proud parents, just like the others.

Hema's little brother had just learnt to walk. He was thrilled to see Hema in a unique Army uniform. He took her military headgear. Hema was equally thrilled to play with him. She had given him the nickname Kika Commando.

Hema had her first posting in Jammu and Kashmir. Her job was quite challenging in several parts of Kashmir. She used to phone home whenever she had time in the evening.

Following her posting, she faced a number of extremist attacks. She was involved in the killings of several militants. She became well-known as super commando in her army unit.

Her father used to ask Hema to leave her job if it was too difficult for her. But Hema was really content there. She enjoys tough things.

After a year of her posting, she was assigned to a special unit that dealt with militant activity. She and her teammates were sent to a secret location for training. Everyone picked for this training was not permitted to communicate with their relatives until the training was completed.

Mohit became concerned for Hema when she did not contact home for a few months. Mohit attempted to obtain information on Hema, but received no information regarding her whereabouts.

His wife tried to persuade him that she might have been dispatched on a secret mission and would be back at the headquarter location soon. His parents and Tanya's parents agreed that Hema was safe and would return shortly.

One day, Tanya's parents encounter a girl who resembles Hema while visiting a tourist attraction. She was strolling on foot with a young guy.

For a minute, Tanya's parents believed they had located Hema. They became enraged and shouted, "You're having fun here, and everyone back home is worried about you. Why didn't you call home over the last few weeks? Your father is anxious about you. Is everything all right with you? Who is this boy?" Tanya's father inquired.

That girl looked around and inquired, "Are you talking to me?"

"Yes, I am asking you. What are you doing here? You are enjoying your holidays here with this boy," Tanya's father said.

"Grandpa, I apologize. You're probably mistaken. I'm not your grandchild. My name is Aamiya George. I have recently joined as sub-inspector in the town," the girl replied.

"Don't be clever. You are making excuses because you are caught with this boy," said Tanya's father.

He then sought for the locket around her neck. She wore the same locket as Hema did. He was convinced she was Hema.

"Do not make a mockery of ourselves. We are certain you are Hema, and you have fled your army duties. You have produced this new boy hair-cut because you feared that we might identify you and come to know of your cowardly deed," Tanya's father said.

Hearing the name "Hema", Aamiya realized what was going on.

"Grandpa, I understand your position. It is not your fault. I was equally shocked when I met Hema in Goa. She looks exactly like me," Aamiya explained.

"She's your granddaughter! I see." Aamiya exclaimed. She smiled sweetly and walked away.

"You can't be our Zeta Commando. My Zeta is a brave girl," said Tanya's father.

The girl halted her trek and returned to the irate grandpa.

"How did you know Zeta Commando?" she asked.

"You informed us your name is Zeta Commando during the airplane hijack situation," Grandpa explained.

Aamiya stood perplexed and startled for a while. She didn't understand how Grandpa knew about Zeta commando. She couldn't recall telling anyone about her name, Zeta. Only she and several of her close friends were aware that she used to have a card with a watermark of Greek letter 'ζ'.

She stopped for a few moments, as if she was about to declare that she was Hema. She was stunned and had no idea what to say. She decided to leave the place and return to her home.

Tanya's parents returned home. They informed Hema's parents and grandparents of the incident of meeting Hema. Nobody was prepared to accept Hema was there with a boy. Mohit was confident that Hema couldn't do this with him. She might have told him about the boy.

Everyone at home, even Mohit, was bewildered and concerned about Hema. Mohit assumed that girl with a boy was Hema's identical twin sister based on a police probe into the school attack. However. he did not share this with anyone else.

In couple of weeks after this occurrence, Hema completed her training and returned to her base camp with the rest of her team.

After returning to her base camp, Hema contacted home. Everyone was ecstatic at home.

Tanya's parents learned that Hema was undergoing a special training at a hidden location. They were taken aback and wondered who the girl was they had met at the tourist attraction.

Tanya's parents could not forget that occurrence of meeting a girl resembling Hema at the tourist site. They were concerned about how it may be possible, given the same locket was on the girl's neck. They felt the girl might be Hema's twin sister.

Tayna's father said to his wife, "Only that nurse might know the actual truth. We need to locate her."

"It will be quite difficult to find her now," stated his wife.

He began searching for the nurse who had helped the family during Tanya's pregnancy. After a few days of searching, they were successful in finding her. Tanya's father's appearance stunned the nurse.

"I knew you'd come back one day. When you can't find solutions to some questions, you'll definitely look for me," stated the nurse.

Tanya's father inquired as to her well-being.

"I am very fine. What about you?," replied the nurse.

"I am also fine. But I'm totally lost," he added.

"Could you tell me the truth about Tanya's pregnancy?" requested Tanya's father.

"Have you found both of the girls?" inquired the nurse.

Tanya's father asked, "What do you mean by the girls?"

"I knew there were twins in Tanya's womb before she gave birth," the nurse said. "But I kept it a secret because you had decided not to keep the child and instead leave it at the entrance of some shrine."

"As soon as the infants were delivered, I handed one to a couple who were unable to have their own baby," Nurse explained.

"This wonderful couple suffered several miscarriages. Doctors had advised the couple not to conceive because the mother was unfit to have a kid. Doctors also advised them to have their baby through IVF and surrogacy, but they couldn't afford the expenses," the nurse added.

"Thank you so much for this kid act," Tanya's father added.

"I'm sure that girl is doing well in her life," the nurse remarked.

"You have protected me from committing the sin of double murder. By God's grace, both girls are fine," Tanya's father stated. "One has already united with her birth mother."

That nurse was startled to hear it and thanked God because she had felt guilty her entire life since their birth.

"Are you in contact with that couple?" Tanya's father inquired.

"I was in contact with that couple for several years. However, after their deaths in a car accident, the girl was placed in an orphanage because no relatives came to care for her. She suffered multiple injuries in that accident, but she survived. I used to visit her and care for her while she was in the hospital. She was a fighting tiger. After she was discharged from the hospital, an orphanage somewhere in Punjab took over her care. After that, I have no idea where she is," The Nurse said.

Tanya's father thanked the nurse before leaving for home. One of Tanya's father's unanswered questions was regarding the identical locket that girl wore. He proceeded to the goldsmith's store, where he had ordered the particular locket. He had expected the locket to be unique, as promised by the goldsmith.

The goldsmith was not at the shop. He looked around the shop and asked, "Would you call Dilbagh Verma? Please." "I want to talk to him."

"He's no more. He departed us a few years back. I'm his son, Rohit Verma," replied the young guy in the store.

He requested his store servant to fetch him water and tea.

"What's the matter, Uncle? May I assist you?" Rohit Verma said.

"Thank you. But I don't think you can help in this situation. I made a specifically crafted locket from this shop several years ago. Your father had promised me it would be unique and would not be sold to anybody else. It was my special design," Tanya's father said.

"It's difficult to say if it was sold to someone else or not. I apologize," Rohit Verma said.

Just as Tanya's father was preparing to leave the shop, Raju, an old servant, arrived. Tanya's father recognized him and quickly exclaimed, "He might know about it!"

"Do you recognize me?" He asked Raju.

"Yes, Uncle. How are you?" Raju stated.

"Do you recall that I made a particular locket from this shop?" He asked Raju.

"Yes, I remember it vividly. It was a unique design," Raju explained.

"Has it been sold to anyone else?" Tanya's father questioned Raju.

"Actually, you arrived one week late to collect your locket. In the meantime, a couple arrived who were expecting their first child after several years. They were looking for something special for their child. While seeking for something unusual, they came across your locket in a package," Raju stated.

"Dilbagh uncle refused to sell it to them. However, they insisted and became emotional. Finally, Dilbagh sold it to them and requested them not to tell anyone. Dilbagh uncle had to manufacture a new one for you," Raju explained.

Tanya's father was overjoyed to learn everything about it and returned home. He thanked God for His generosity and for saving both girls. He told his wife everything, but he didn't dare to inform Tanya about her second daughter.

Tanya's father was finally convinced that Aamiya was Hema's twin sister.

One day, Mohit paid a visit to Tanya's parents.

"Can I share something with you? You may hate me after hearing it," Tanya's father told Mohit.

"Did you recall what I told you about a girl who looked like Hema?" Tanya's father inquired.

"Yes, I remember," Mohit replied.

"She is Hema's twin sister," Tanya's father said.

"How do you know about it?" said Mohit.

Tanya's father revealed that Hema wears a locket shaped like the letter 'ζ' around her neck. The similar locket hangs around her twin sister's neck. He mentioned that he had manufactured these particularly designed lockets from a goldsmith.

He also said that he was unaware Tanya had given birth to twin girls. While I abandoned one baby girl at a bridge, the nurse gave the other to a couple who couldn't have their own children.

"Oh my God! Where can we meet her?" Mohit inquired.

Tanya's father stated, "She is a sub-inspector in a town in Haryana. Hema and Aamiya had met in Goa a few years ago. However, they are unaware that they are twin sisters."

XIII

Tanya's father was lost in her thoughts, reflecting on the lives of Hema and Aamiya.

Hema was raised as a princess by a loving father, but her twin sister Aamiya grew up in an orphanage. Hema had everything she wanted, and Aamiya had whatever was available in the orphanage. Hema attended one of the city's top private schools, while Aamiya attended one of the city's public schools.

Both twin sisters had a great love for sports and a fascination with defence and police uniforms. They were capable of fighting in self-defense.

One day, Aamiya met Shiv Kumar, a so-called 'Zeta Commando' in the police investigation into an attack on a school campus. He recognized Aamiya's face and shouted 'Zeta'. He was astonished to see her wearing a police uniform.

"Are you a commando? Everyone has been looking for you for so long. Where were you?" He asked Aamiya.

Aamiya was so astonished that she stood dumbfounded for a while.

"I didn't recognize you. Do you know me?" Aamiya asked.

"Do you recall that evening attack in a school? You fought well, killing all the assailants and saving my life," He said.

Aamiya flashed back to the school attack, but she refused to recognise him.

"You're probably mistaken. I joined the police force just a couple of years ago," Aamiya said.

Shiv Kumar speculated that she might be Hema.

"Please show me your neck," said Shiv Kumar.

Aamiya showed him her neck. There was an injury scar on her neck. He was convinced she was 'Zeta Commando'.

"Do you know you have a twin sister?" Shiv Kumar inquired.

"I apologize. I grew up in an orphanage. I don't have any twin sister," She said.

"That could be due to an unfortunate incident, but you have a twin sister who has grown up under the care of a single father," Shiv Kumar explained.

Aamiya somehow began to believe she might have a twin sister.

"Thank you. It was a joy meeting you. See you later," replied Aamiya.

Shiv Kumar found himself repeatedly returning his gaze to Aamiya. He was certain it was the same girl, but he couldn't prove it.

A few days later, a team of three police officers, including Aamiya, was dispatched to apprehend one of the terrorists hiding in a town. There was a tip off that a terrorist had entered the town, but there was no information regarding his appearance or location. He was supposed to be on a big assignment, according to the tip-off.

All of the police officers were dressed in civilian attire, seeking for any clues to learn more about the terrorist. They were living in various hotels. They had no idea who the terrorist was for a few days.

Aamiya learned that a local politician could be involved in harboring the terrorist. She informed her senior officers at the headquarters. But no one believed her, dismissing her information as foolishness. The politician was regarded as a good guy by the public.

Aamiya resolved to confront the politician and went to his house, but his security guards refused to let her in. She requested that she has to meet with him to address an important matter. They notified the politician of her desire again, but he declined.

Aamiya chose to wait some distance away from the politician's residence. While sitting there and eating some snacks, she noticed a person exiting the politician's house in a car; she had a feeling she had seen that person before. While riding her bicycle, she was wondering where she had seen that person. She eventually realized she had seen him beg around town. Aamiya was confident that this person was the terrorist that they were hunting for.

However, the terrorist fled the town before any attempts were made to apprehend him. There was a tip-off that he had gone to another city to hire some young people to complete some big chores. The police squad arrived in that city. This time, he (the terrorist) was driving a cab in town under a fictitious identity during the day and setting up a booth in the evening selling roasted ground nuts. He had been hunting for unemployed teenagers to entice them with money and carry out his plan of attacks at some public places.

In the evening, while roaming in the market, Aamiya saw some youths standing near a stall of roasted groundnuts. She asked for groundnuts for ₹20. She recognized that person selling groundnuts.

As he offered Aamiya groundnuts, he remembered her face as if he had seen her before. He noticed Aamiya calling on her phone, he grew suspicious since he remembered seeing her in another town. He suspected she was an undercover police officer.

He instantly tried to close his stall and flee, but Aamiya was watchful. She caught hold of him and handcuffed him. As soon as her teammates came, he was detained and blindfolded. He was promptly transported to a local police station and thrown in jail. When questioned by a police team, he confessed that a terrorist attack was planned on the railway stations on the next Dussehra. All train station police were instructed to look for anything suspicious or unattended.

After apprehending the terrorist, Aamiya became famous. Her photographs were featured in newspapers and other media platforms.

The police team investigating the terrorist attack on a school summoned Aamiya and confirmed that she was the real Zeta Commando.

Aamiya reavealed that on the day of the terrorist attack, she was in the city to visit a senior retired police officer. He was meant to explain the details of physical testing for police jobs. Aamiya was preparing for her police sub-inspector exam and physical tests.

She was riding her bike and passed a school when she heard a noise. When she arrived, she discovered that several terrorists had held hostages. She looked around as the police prepared to attack. When she observed some commandos going up from the back via a pipe, she put on a commando suit and helmet from a police van and went up with them.

She had a card with a watermark of the Greek letter 'ζ' on it. She somehow misplaced her card while assisting the unconscious commando. She fled the site immediately following the incident, fearing that it might jeopardize her chances of earning a position with the police. She was appointed as a police sub-inspector a couple of years after the incident.

When terrorists learned she was Zeta Commando, who had been bothering them for years and foiled their numerous attempts at public attacks. They were looking for the means to kidnap or kill her.

Hema returned home for a one-month vacation. Her haircut was identical to Aamiya's. It was now difficult to distinguish between Hema and Aamiya just by looking at their faces. The only difference was a scar on Aamiya's neck. Only Shiv Kumar and Hema's father knew about the scar.

Hema learned about an inspector who arrested a dangerous terrorist from newspapers and other media sources.

"Papa!, Have you read the newspapers?" Hema enquired, presenting newspapers to her father.

"Yes, I have read these newspapers," Mohit answered.

"Look at the inspector! Pa. She's the same girl I met in Goa," Hema added.

"She might be your twin sister," Mohit explained. "If you ever meet her again, look for a locket around her neck. She has a locket similar to yours."

"Pa!, How did you find out about it?" Hema inquired.

"This is both unfortunate and mysterious. Your maternal grandfather told me about it," Mohit explained.

Hema felt eager about finding Aamiya. She started searching for Aamiya. Terrorists kidnapped Hema on the mistaken belief that she was Aamiya.

Hema was riding a bicycle alone in the morning, when she was kidnapped by terrorists. She battled the captors, but they were well-prepared and successfully kidnapped her.

When Mohit learned about the kidnapping, he became concerned and went to meet Tanya's father. He asked Tanya's father for assistance.

"We should look for Hema's twin sister," Tanya's father said.

Mohit promptly agreed with Tanya's father. They travelled from town to town in quest of Aamiya George. They were unable to discover her despite a half day search. While returning to their homes in the afternoon, they discovered Hema with a lovely boy in their city. Hema was wearing a cap, and the boy was one of her coworkers in the Indian Army. They mistook her for Aamiya.

"Your twin sister has been kidnapped by terrorists. Nobody knew where she is. We need your help to find her," Tanya's father remarked.

Mohit noticed no scars on her neck and recognized her. He was going to cheer, but Hema gestured with her folded palms and raised eyebrows, as if to beg, "Please don't say anything."

Mohit remained quiet. Hema declined to assist and requested them to go home because she was occupied with some vital responsibilities.

"I don't have a twin sister. Don't try to make a fool of me," Hema murmured, folding her hands and smiling. "I apologize. Please trust me."

Tanya's father said, "I separated you both at birth." He cried and pleaded with Hema.

"I'm sorry, Grandpa, but I can't help you. Please leave me alone. I'll meet you in the evening and chat to you about what you're saying. Give me your address." Hema requested.

Mohit offered his business card. Tanya's father began crying. Hema then waved her hand to her father and went away.

"Mohit, go home, and I'll come after some rest," Tanya's father remarked.

Mohit returned home and questioned Tanya, "Where's Hema?"

"She went to the city to meet some of her friends," Tanya replied.

"Did you know she has an identical twin sister? She has the same appearance as Hema. It is impossible to distinguish between them," stated Tanya.

"I had learned about it from a police team, but I had no idea where she was. I didn't know if she was alive or dead," Mohit added.

He became remorseful to Tanya. Tanya became distraught and took Mohit inside Hema's bedroom. Aamiya was asleep there. Mohit showed Tanya her identity symbol, a scar on her neck. A police commando who survived a terrorist strike at a school has told him everything. She is widely known as Zeta Commando.

Mohit informed Tanya that they met Hema in the city, but your father mistook her as Aamiya.

"When your father gets home, you should pretend you don't know anything about Hema and Aamiya," Mohit requested Tanya.

Tanya's father arrived home in the evening, looking exhausted and dejected.

"I couldn't save your daughter. She has been kidnapped by some terrorists," Tanya's father told her. He began crying uncontrollably. Tanya also began crying.

"Papa! I learned from Mohit that I had given birth to twin girls," Tanya remarked. "You separated all of us from each other."

"I deeply regret this occurrence," Tanya's father said. "I can't explain why I did that."

In the meantime, Aamiya emerges from Hema's bedroom. Tanya's father went to hug Aamiya, mistaking her for Hema, and began crying again.

"Thank God you're safe and have returned home," he replied.

Everyone sat in the living room, but there was perfect stillness for some time.

Aamiya went inside to speak with her mother in the kitchen. In the meantime, Hema returned home. She knocked on the door and said, "May I come in."

"Hello, Grandpa! Where is my twin sister?" asked Hema.

Grandpa was upset and angry since she refused to help them. He still assumed she was Aamiya.

"Why have you come now? By the grace of God, she has safely returned home," remarked Grandpa.

"Grandpa, God is always with us. He always treats us well. You were overly concerned," replied Hema.

Tanya's father noticed an injury mark on her forehead.

"What happened? Did you fight with someone?" Tanya's father questioned Hema.

"Small conflicts are typical in the police force. It's part of our job," Hema explained.

Grandpa now grinned and hugged Hema, still believing she was Aamiya.

"Your twin sister is inside. You should be proud of her. She is an officer in the Indian army. You go inside and meet her," Tanya's father stated.

Hema went in. Aamiya was in the kitchen with her mother, cooking food.

When Hema and Aamiya emerge together. Hema had removed her headgear. Tanya's father had a tough time distinguishing between Hema and Aamiya.

Hema and Aamiya sat on a sofa near Tanya's father's chair. He was frozen, as if looking at Hema and Aamiya.

"Pa, can you identify between Hema and Aamiya?" Tanya questioned her father. "You encountered Hema in the city today. Aamiya was sleeping at home and only woke up when you arrived."

"How did Aamiya and Hema find each other?" Tanya's father inquired.

"Pa, I don't know this. But when Hema brought Aamiya home, we were all astonished to see them together," Tanya explained.

"Hema and Aamiya have sustained slight injuries. Tanya began to cry when she saw two similar Hema together. She couldn't believe the vision of two similar girls. She held her girls and grieved all she could. She cleansed blood from her daughters' minor injuries," Tanya's mother shared.

Tanya was upset with her parents, but she also thought that everything happened as God intended. There must be some good in there.

One day, Mohit's entire family, including Aamiya and Tanya's parents, went on a picnic to a hill station. On the way, Aamiya described the events surrounding the kidnapping of Hema.

That day, Aamiya had come to the city for some official assignment. She was riding her bike when she noticed some people roughly forcing a girl into a van. She paused for a moment and remembered that the girl in the van was Hema. Aamiya followed the van for some distance before they began firing. She abruptly used the brakes, causing her bike to skid. She received some minor injuries. This is when she became suspicious and discovered they'd kidnapped Hema.

As a police officer, it was her obligation to rescue her from them.

However, before Aamiya arrived, Hema had managed to overpower her kidnappers. She had slain one, and executing flawless taekwondo kicks on the others.

Aamiya felt her breath hitch. It was like watching herself in a mirror.

Hema turned, wiping her forehead. Her gaze met Aamiya's.

And she froze.

For a long moment, neither of them spoke. The air between then crackled with something unspoken, unknown, yet undeniable

Aamiya's eyes narrowed. "You…" she whispered. "You're the girl from Goa."

Hema swallowed hard. "Yes. But I am more than that."

Aamiya took a cautious step forward. "What do you mean?"

Hema's voice wavered. "I think… no, I know that we are sisters."

Aamiya's breath caught.

"That's impossible," she said, but there was doubt in her voice.

"You grew up in an orphanage. You never understood why you felt... different," Hema continued.

Aamiya's jaw tightened. "How do you know all this?"

"I have this, ʒ-shaped locket," Hema said softly. "And... so do you."

Aamiya's eyes widened. Her hand instinctively moved to her own neck, where the same ʒ-shaped locket hung.

The world around them seemed to stand still.

Two sisters. Separated by fate. Reunited by destiny.

Aamiya let out a shaky breath.

Hema stepped closer.

"You," she whispered, "are the real Zeta Commando."

Silence.

Then, in a blur, Aamiya lunged forward and wrapped her arms around Hema. Holding her as if she had found a missing piece of herself.

Hema hugged her back, her throat tightening.

For the first time in her life, she wasn't alone.

And neither was Aamiya.

XIV

Following Aamiya's posting in the city, where Mohit's family resided, Aamiya began living with her mother and sister. She now has loving parents and grandparents. She had notified her orphanage that she had located her birth mother and twin sister. She thanked her God for reuniting them all.

Mohit was proud of his large family. He was thankful to God for all of his blessings and for reuniting the twin daughters with their mother.

"I am overjoyed to be joined with you both. I am really proud of you both. At the same time, I am deeply sorry that I was unable to shower you both with motherly affection," Tanya stated.

"Come on, mom! Whatever happens is always good. It is all under His wish," Aamiya added.

"Why were you both called Zeta yourself?" Tanya inquired.

"Because of this locket, which was in the form of a Greek letter Zeta 'ζ,'" Hema explained.

Tanya's father was overjoyed but apologetic to Tanya and her daughters.

Everyone in their neighborhood and at work refers to Hema as well as Aamiya as Zeta Commando.

The name 'Zeta Commando' became synonymous with resolving outstanding problems in their community, and at work.

One day, Aamiya got shocked to discover a file in which about 11 unsolved death mysteries due to a poison were reported.

"Oh my God! This bloody mystery has to be solved," she said to herself.

She thoroughly studied that file and decided to resolve the mystery. All the youths died in these cases were linked to a businessman's family. The police investigations of all of these deaths indicate the invelovement of the businessman's family. This businessman has been himself a cabinet minister in the previous government.

Nobody had ever dared to arrest any member of businessman's family although everbody believes his family is involved in all these mysterius deaths.

"How the hell is he not in jail? He has to pay for his deeds," said Aamiya.

Several police teams were made to work on this mystery. These teams went to different places and searched all the known industrial plants linked to the businessman. Many of the illegal businesses of the businessman were exposed.

In some of industrial plants, drugs were produced and sold illigally in the market. The businessman was very angry. He threatened Aamiya for serious consequences if she took any action against his family members. He also used to boast of those mysterious deaths to threaten the police officers.

When details of illegal businesses were reported in the news papers, the supporters of the businessman created a chaos in the city.

"It is a conspirancy to defame our leader," said his supporters. "Our leader is innocent."

Aamiya along with some of her colleagues went to meet the businessman.

"We are doing our duty. If you have nothing to do with all those illegal businesses, ask your people not to destroy the public property and have patience," said Aamiya to the businessman.

"Soon you will discover more details about me. Either you will be shifted to some other place or you will be gone...," said the angry businessman.

"I am not scared of anything. I have taken the pledge of implementing the constitution," said Aamiya. "Wait for the day I find some concrete evidence against you."

The samples collected from different business places and industrial plants of the businessman were sent to a lab for examination. However, that poison was not found in any of the chemical samples collected from different industrial plants.

"Either this businessman has nothing to do with those deaths or there is some more hidden places of his illegal activities," said Aamiya.

Hema had come home for one month vacation, and was having great time with her parents, grandparents and siblings.

"Aamiya! How are you?" Hema asked, one evening.

"I'm fine. I have got to resolve a very serious case," said Aamiya. "I have got a file related to the mysterious deaths of several victims in last one and half years."

"Death mysteries? Is it related to the deaths due to a poison?"asked Hema.

Aamiya stood awestruck for a while and did not understood what to say. After a while, Aamiya asked,"How did you know about these deaths?"

"We are army officers," said Hema with a big amile on her face.

"It is a case of 11 mysterious deaths over the period of one year due to some unknwon poison. During my last vacations, I got the information that a terrorist has entered in the city. He was infamous as a death merchant. I was looking for him and to find out if he has any involvement in any deaths in the city. That time, a police officer told me that a businessman's family was involved in all those deaths according to the investigations by the police department," Hema stated.

"Oh my God!," Aamiya saluted Hema. "You are a great Army officer. I love you," Aamiya hugged Hema kissed her on her cheeks.

"It was the same terrorist that was arrested by you," Hema remarked.

"I accept you as my teacher, please train me," said Aamiya with her folded hands.

"Undoudbtly, the businessman's family was involved in several deaths but in all of these mysteious deaths due to a poison, his family has no involvement in my investigation," said Hema. "It is the work of a geneous who has never been a suspect in the police investigations."

"Does the businessman's family know this culprit?" asked Aamiya.

"Probably, yes. But they don't know he/she is the culprit behind these deaths. It is someone who has somehow developed this poison in his/her personal lab and has grudge with the businessman's family?," said Hema.

Aamiya was quietly listoning to Hema, thinking that she had already resolved the mystery.

"There was a boy whose whereabouts are not known. He had gone to Germany to pursue his Ph.D degree in biochemistry.

All members of his family died in an election violence instigated by supporters of the businessman, who had filed her candidature in an assembly election. I doubt he could be one of the suspects." Hema added further.

"You are already so close to solve this mystery," stated Aamiya.

"Not yet," said Hema. "But it will be solved soon. Now you have got to find out where is that genious guy."

"Thank you so much, Hema. I want to be like you. You are genious like James Bond," said Aamiya.

Hema shared some of her service tips with Aamiya.

"Along with doing your job, it is also important to enjoy life and stress out yourself taking short breaks with family,"Hema advised to Aamiya.

She shared with Aamiya some of her army training skills and psychology of troubling youths.

XV

While sitting in her office, Aamiya was thinking about that the elusive guy suspected to be involved in those mysterious deaths due to a poison.

And then, she got the news that a terrorist, captured by her and her colleagues a few months ago, escaped from jail.

"This bloody merchant of death should be gunned down on the spot," Aamiya said in desperation. "I won't spare him this time, rather kill him on the spot."

Aamiya along with two of her colleagues visited a railway station. She noticed two suspecious youths came on a bike. She stopped them at the entrance. They got scared and tried to run away, throwing their bag.

However, Aamiya and her colleagues were allert and grabed both the youths. They revealed that they had come to deliver a consignment to someone waiting at the railway station.

They were taken to a police station. Aamiya was hoping to get some clue about the escaped terrorist and the source of mysterious poison.

"There is someone who is trying to create and smuggle deadly tiny insects into the cities in India," revealed one of the youths.

"Oh my God! That would be desastrous. It could be some deadly viruses or bacteria," exclaimed Aamiya. "Where is this bloody idiot merchant of death?".

"We do not know anything, except that we heard our handler saying that Mr Khan is creating deadly minute creatures which will be smuggled soon into the cities in India," said another youth.

Nobody knew about Mr Khan, except that he was working against humanity and looking to create his own world.

"Our handler gave us work and in return we get some money. We are both post graduates, but there is no job," the youth further added.

Hearing this, Aamiya slapped both the youths. "Just for money, you are spoiling lives of other's children."

Aamiya suspected that the escaped terrorist might knew the location of Mr Khan. She flashed back a past incident— she had recognised the escaped terrorist after visiting a politician's home.

"That politician might have helped the terrorist to escape and hide somewhere," Aamiya remarked to herself. She decided to visit him again.

"I came here to allert you that a terrorist has escaped. In case, you get any information, inform us immediately," Aamiya remarked.

"Why would he come here? He might have escaped to Kashmir," the politician said.

Hearing it, Aamiya was convinced that he certainly knew where is that terrorist. She turned towards him and gazed him for a while, but did not say anything. She looked around for anything suspicious.

Aamiya decided to came back home, riding her bike. She noticed looking in the rear mirror of her bike that two cars were following her. She got suspicious and changed her route. She decided to stop near a restaurent. After a while, those people arrived searching for her.

They looked around and asked, "Did some young girl come here?"

The people eating in the restaurent suddenly started looking towards them. In the meantime, there were gun shots outside. The people eating in the restaurent got scared and run for hiding in corners or behind some obstacles whatever they could find. The people looking for Aamiya came running towards their cars and found one tyre each of their cars punctured.

"Who did this?" they shouted and got ready with their deadly weapons they had brought with themselves.

Aamiya was observing the situation in hiding behind a tree. She shot most of them bin the leg. When she was sure that they can't chase her anymore. She took her bike and left the scene.

These people were sent by the politician. When they came back injured, he become very angry.

One evening, Hema and Aamiya decided to visit a bustling shopping mall. As they wandered through the aisles, browsing different stores, Hema's eyes fell on a woman wearing long gloves that reached up to her elbows. Something about her demeanor struck Hema as odd, but she couldn't immediately place why.

Later, inside the changing room of a boutique, Hema happened to notice the same woman removing her right glove. To her shock, the woman's right hand had no fingers. A cold shiver ran down her spine as she recalled a critical detail from an ongoing investigation. The prime suspect behind a series of mysterious deaths was rumored to have lost fingers in an accident years ago. "Could this be the same person?" she whispered.

Heart pounding, Hema immediately informed Aamiya. They discreetly followed the woman through the mall, carefully observing her every move. Their pursuit led them to a dimly lit cafe where the woman took a secluded seat. Hema and Aamiya watched as she sipped her drink, seemingly lost in thought. Gathering their courage, they decided to confront her.

When questioned, the woman initially maintained a calm exterior, claiming she was simply a scientist who had left her previous life behind. However, when further investigated, shocking revelations came to light. The woman was, in fact, a transgender individual who had disappeared from the public eye two years ago. Before her transition, she had been a brilliant scientist named Dr Ankur Goyal, known for his expertise in biochemistry.

Upon arrest and during interrogation, she finally broke down and confessed. She revealed that she had spent the past two years meticulously planning her revenge. Her targets were not random; they were individuals who had wronged her in the past. She had developed a lethal heavy metal poison that slowly caused clotting in the bloodstream, leading to cardiac arrest within 20 to 24 hours. Her method of delivery was ingenious—she had designed a custom artificial hand that housed a retractable, nearly undetectable syringe. With a simple handshake or a light touch, she could inject her victims without raising suspicion.

A few days later, the city was under siege. Some masked attackers, sent by Mr Khan, stormed a government building, taking hostages. Armed police surrounded the area, negotiating, but everyone knew—it wouldn't end peacefully.

Hema and Aamiya stood on a rooftop nearby, dressed in tactical gear. Identical. Synchronized. Fighting together for the first time.

Aamiya loaded her gun.

Hema smirked, "You saved me once. It's my turn now."

Aamiya glanced at her twin. "You're not scared?"

Hema grinned. "No. Because this time, I'm not figthing alone."

They moved like shadows, slipping through the back entrance of the building.

Silent.

Deadly.

Unstaoppable.

Inside, the terrorists were on high alert. They had no idea that two ghosts—two warriors—were already hunting them.

A terrorist turned, spoting movement. "Who's there?"

Hema dropped low, sweeping his legs. Before he could even scream, Aamiya had him in a chokhold. He slumped to the ground, unconsious.

One down.

They moved forward, their minds working as one. No words are needed.

Through an open door, they spoted the hostages—ties up, terrified. The leaders of the attackers stood in front, barking threats into a phone.

Aamiya's fingers curled into fists. "We take them down fast. No room for mistakes."

Hema nodded. "You go high, I go low."

A single breath.

Then—they moved.

Aamiya lauched herself from a desk, flipping through the air. The leader's eyes widened—too low. She slammed a kick into his jaw, knocking him out cold.

At the same time, Hema rolled across the floor, grabbing a fallen pistol. Three shots—perfectly placed. Lights out for the rest of the attackers.

Silence.

The hostages stared in shock. "Who are these commandos, looking as if cloned?"

"Cops are coming. We need to vanish," Hema said.

Aamiya smirked, "Again?"

Hema shrugged, "Some things never change."

As the sirens blared outside, the Zeta Commandos disappeared into the shadows.

The legend of Zeta Commando would live on.

Only now—it wasn't just one.

It was two.

Zeta Commando adventures to be continued in the
upcoming book,

"Zeta Commandos and the Merchants of Death"